Mary

Anth<

This book is dedicated to my late friend, Tony Byrne, a mentor to many and the epitome of a good, honest and solid British cop.

future, but for all their efforts of attempting to remain upbeat, neither could hide their sadness and concerns for each other.

Following Melanie checking in, Dutch accompanied her to the departures gate and both were tearful as they kissed and said their goodbyes with Dutch stating, "I will remain as long as I can because I don't want to let anyone down here, because I consider that they have been very good to us and really helped me out of a very tight spot. Having said that, if you need me to come home quickly, I will not hesitate to drop everything and get back some way or another."

"I know that you would try, but how you could do that without getting arrested goodness only knows. Once I've seen my parents, we will have to work out a way to be together again. Perhaps, we could all move to another part of England? The Lake District for example, we all so loved those holidays there."

Dutch, attempting to hold back his emotions, said in short staccato bursts, "That's a nice thought to be going on with. You never know I might just surprise you with a happy solution one day, and this nightmare situation will be over forever."

Melanie pulled a small white handkerchief from her sleeve, wiping the tears from his and her own eyes, they then kissed before she entered the departure lounge, and following a final wave she disappeared from his sight.

Dutch, knowing his wife's flight schedule, tracked her return journey to the UK, whilst all the time trying to imagine the sights and sounds that she was experiencing, wishing he was with her doing the same.

One evening following his workday, Dutch entered the car park situated under the main building of the complex. He placed out some miscellaneous obstacles around the concrete surface, constructed the collapsible cane, put on the recently purchased sunglasses, then after switching off the lights he attempted to locate and manoeuvre around the obstacles with the aid of his stick. He had only been engaged in the practice for a few minutes when the lights came on, and at the same time he heard George's voice shout out, "Shit Dutch, what the fuck are you playing at?"

Dutch, feeling somewhat embarrassed at the predicament that he found himself in, replied, "Just practising something. I will tell you all about it one day."

Thankfully for Dutch, George appeared to be in a hurry, and after gathering some spanners from a tool chest positioned in the corner of the car park, shouted, "You Brits have some weird ways of passing the time."

Despite his remarks, once George had extinguished the lights Dutch continued in the engagement of his strange experiment.

Only four days after receiving a text from Melanie informing him that she had arrived safely, and that her parents and Jodie were all fit and well and ecstatic to see her, Dutch received a mobile telephone call from his wife. Her tone of voice immediately concerned him when she said, "I hope that I'm not being paranoid, but something's happened here that I'm concerned about."

"Melanie your tone of voice is worrying me. What's happened, are you or someone else ill?"

"No, nothing like that. Do you remember what you said to me just before you left for Venezuela, while I was still staying with Mum and Dad?"

"Do you mean about being cautious regarding as to what we say during our telephone conversations. I can remember telling you time and time again to be careful, as I was told that a certain group was capable of tracing anyone if they wanted to. I told you so many times that you said I was continually repeating myself. By the way are you using a new mobile that nobody else is aware of?"

"Yes, I got it as soon as I got back. It's nothing like that though, it's more of a feeling I may be being watched."

His voice then rose an octave, "God. Don't tell me that they have located where you are living. Please don't tell me that when I'm stuck out here."

"I'm not sure. It may just be a coincidence but when I was coming back from the shops, walking up Cowley Drive with Jodie this afternoon. I looked to my right into the close just before Mum and Dad. Do you know where I mean?"

"Yes, I know the close, I used to park their sometimes if I couldn't park outside your parents' place."

"Well as I glanced in there, I saw a black shiny Range Rover or similar. I suppose it was the distinctive foreign number plates that made me take an interest, and I remembered that you told me to watch out for any foreign cars around this area."

"It's odd to see foreign cars around there, but it might not be connected."

"But there's more. As I came around the corner, I seemed to surprise three men standing together on the pavement opposite Mum and Dad's. They all quickly looked away when they saw me, which I thought was odd. So, as I walked into my parents' drive, I turned around suddenly and caught them all looking at me and talking quietly. Because I turned, they all then pretended to be looking at a car parked nearby which I know has nothing to do with any of them at all, because it belongs to Jesse next door. Am I just putting two and two together and making more of it then I should?"

"I don't like the sound of this. What did these men look like?"

"Two were dark, dressed smart casual, one taller than the other. The third one was the bloke who lives in the bungalow opposite. He's a right drunk now. Dad told me that he was once a successful businessman until he lost his licence and hit the booze."

"Did you see where they all went to after you went in?"

"I was careful that they didn't see me watching from the front room window. After a few minutes chatting and continually glancing at our place, the bloke living opposite went indoors. The other two walked down the road towards that close and only seconds later that black car drove out onto our road towards the junction of the main road."

"I hate to say this Melanie, but this appears to be more than a coincidence. You have only been home for a short time and it would appear that you have got some men, possibly foreigners, watching you or the property. If they are something to do with the gang connected to what happened to you, the only way that they could have known of your connection with your parents' address is if they have been sniffing about asking questions in the right places. I don't like the sound of this. From what you have told me, we can have more than a reasonable guess that this neighbour could well be involved. What do you know about this supposed drunk?"

"Dad told me they don't see a lot of him, only when he emerges each day about lunchtime when he goes down the shop and returns shortly after with a bag containing mostly alcohol by all accounts. His wife apparently left him some time ago, and I'm not surprised as if you remember that TV comedy character, Rab C Nesbitt, he looks and speaks with the same slurred Scottish accent and staggers about like him. Very often, he is just wearing a vest in all weathers, but minus the headband."

"I remember Rab C Nesbitt. Christ, he must be in a state then! He sounds just the sort who could easily be recruited to report on our movements. If you see that car again clock the number plate and its country of origin."

"Okay Dennis, but is this ever going to end? What shall I do? It's not only me in danger. My parents could become involved?"

"Firstly, don't panic or do anything unusual, because if that bloke over the road is their lookout he may notice. I don't think you or your parents are targets. You know I wouldn't want anything to harm you or your mum and dad, who I have always considered as the parents I never had. It's me that they want, and they will think as you are back, I won't be far behind and will be ready for me. I had a backup plan should anything like this happen, so please listen carefully."

"I'm glad you have a plan as I have no idea what to do now."

"Listen carefully. You remember our conversation just before you left about that really nice holiday cottage that we once rented together with your mum and dad in the Lake District. The owners, who are in the address book, have two similar cottages around there, and I'm sure as it's not holiday season yet, at least one will be vacant, and both are dog friendly. It will be a bit of a shock for your parents, but it's essential that you persuade them to cancel any arrangements and appointments. Tell them that you want to treat them to a holiday to celebrate your return home, or a similar story. While you are all there, why don't you sound them out as to moving there, all of us, like we have discussed in the past? If they show an interest, consider looking around at properties with annexes and prices. We must all get away from the South and these re-occurring problems."

"God Dennis, this is all hard to take in. I do like the idea of moving up there while Mum and Dad are fit enough to enjoy it, but springing it on me like this is a bit much."

"I know it is, and I appreciate how difficult it is for you to do, but you need to do this straight away, but don't whatever you do let that bloke over the road see you go. You will have to leave discreetly. I don't foresee too many problems with your parents, they loved those holidays and always wanted to go back there. They are still only in their mid-sixties and both in relatively good health. You will all have to go in your dad's car as it's far bigger than your Fiat. If he doesn't fancy driving all that distance perhaps you can do a stint. By the way, is the Fiat still going okay?"

"Yes, it's fine, as Dad has been looking after it in our absence. Of course, I may find driving a bit difficult at first, as I have only done a little bit since being back, but I'm sure I will manage. He will certainly look forward to doing some fishing, so I don't foresee any objections from him."

"I'm glad that you mentioned fishing as somewhere amongst his tackle your dad has a catapult, could you ask him to dig it out for me and leave it in the shed?"

"Did I hear you correctly Dennis? You want Dad's catapult? I know that you got rid of the gun, and I was glad of that, but what an earth are you going to do with a catapult even if you do get back? You tell me that these men are serious gangsters and the next minute you think you are going to protect us with a piece of elastic."

"Don't be silly, I'm not going to fire it at them, but it may assist me in getting rid of them once and for all."

"Dennis, I do worry about you and your madcap ideas."

His thoughts turned to the Walther PPK 9mm pistol that she was referring to which he had used to dispose of the two responsible for raping and assaulting his wife and attempting to rape another woman in the same manner. He had found the weapon while serving in Kosovo, which he had smuggled into the UK as a trophy amongst a vast amount of military equipment and had successfully concealed it close to his home. Following shooting the assailants he had broken down the weapon and disposed of both parts and ammunition from a footbridge into the river that flowed beneath. How he needed it now but it would have been remiss to have retained such damming evidence linking him to the crime.

"It will all turn out fine, I'm sure. Book the cottage for at least two weeks, then wait to hear from me, so always have your mobile on and fully charged. If you can do this, I'm pretty confident I can sort this mess out one way or another."

"Oh God, I do hope so; although, how you are going to do it while over there, or in police custody, I don't know. Just be careful whatever you do, and don't do anything stupid, please. Wouldn't it be easier for me to report my suspicions to the police, perhaps they could help? After all it might turn out to be nothing. Or try to persuade Mum and Dad to sell up and move up there as quick as we can."

"We can't take any chances, as this gang are ruthless, not Mickey Mouse villains but the real deal. If they have continued to take an interest in me for this long, they are obviously hell-bent on revenge. They have somehow traced you this time, so could probably do the same again. So I need to finalise this. Informing the police did briefly cross my mind, but what if they don't take it seriously? After all, you are the wife of a man suspected of killing five people, so they may have little sympathy with your predicament that you may or may not be in. If they do get involved and try to put them off of doing anything, or they mount an operation but show out to them, gangsters like them will just lay low and try again another day. There is also a possibility that the police will prolong the situation and, in a similar way, use you as bait in the hope that I will return to protect you. If that happens, even if hopefully I am only banged up on remand for a short period, I won't be around for you. I was warned that this firm will not give up if anyone crossed them, as they like to show all that they can't be messed with, and if someone does, they never give up until they have settled a score."

"I hear what you say, Dennis. You are right. We need to get away from here quickly, while you try to sort something out, but goodness knows how you are going to do that. Whatever you do, just be careful. I love you and couldn't ever do without you, despite all of this. I just wish I could have been strong enough to go to court and this would never have happened."

"Don't go beating yourself up again. You were in no mental state to testify in court, and anyway jail was too good for every one of those scumbags. I have no regrets for what I did, as I did the world a favour, but unfortunately the law won't see it that way. My only regret is what it is now doing to you and your parents. Now we must both get cracking. Let me know if you have any problems with those arrangements. Whatever you do, don't let that geezer opposite see you go. I alone got us all into this mess and I will in some way or the other get us out of it. Oh! I nearly forgot, if I do get back could you put your keys to the bungalow, garage and shed in the usual place in the garden where you have left them for me before?"

"I will make sure they are there. Imagine if you were lucky enough to get all the way here and then find yourself locked out!"

"I can cope with being locked out, but I'm not getting locked up if I can help it. Whatever you do, don't forget what I asked about the catapult. Love you, bye."

Although, he had remained as calm as possible so as not to alarm Melanie, inside his emotions were running wild, further exasperated by the distance and obstructions keeping them apart. He knew that if members of the gang were watching Melanie, if he didn't follow quickly they may lose patience, either possibly kidnapping or harming her in an effort to force his return. A simple unprepared moving home was not going to stop the threat. He would never tell Melanie, but he considered that he would be looking over his shoulder for the rest of his days. Melanie had been his first serious girlfriend, who he had known since the age of seventeen, and such thoughts brought back guilty memories of his one and only transgression during their long and happy relationship. They were married, when as a young soldier he together with colleagues went on a stag weekend to Warrington in Cheshire. During the evening, by chance, he met an attractive woman named Kerry, which subsequently led to a night of frantic love-making. Melanie had never discovered his unfaithfulness and he had been consumed with guilt ever since. He couldn't even put the blame on drink as he had been stone-cold sober. It was a guilty secret that he found difficult to deal with, but he would never tell her as they had been through so much together, it would break her heart.

As soon as the call terminated, an extremely concerned Dutch calmed himself and speed dialled the number which his former boss, Mr Chamberlain had given him.

Chamberlain answered, and Dutch explained that he must return to the UK immediately due to a family emergency, with little chance of him returning to Venezuela. Chamberlain understood his predicament and stated that he would honour his previous promise and find an immediate replacement, ensuring that he received any wages owed to him before his departure.

Having authorised his leaving, Dutch approached Holton and informed him of his immediate plans. Holton stated that he was sorry to see him go but thought it was only a matter of time after Melanie's departure. Dutch asked him not to mention his intended leaving to George and Bo, as he wished to inform them himself.

From that moment, due to his concern for Melanie and her parents, he sprung into full exit mode. His first task was to gather together his own passport and other personal documents bearing his name. Together with a brief note, he posted them by express delivery to his sister Jeanette at her Brighton address; requesting her to look after them along with a package that he had ordered from a UK army surplus store. His next step was to engage in a Google search to identify specialists at the London eye hospital, followed by a telephone call to the hospital enquiring as to particular specialists' usual working week. Dutch soon received the answer that he had anticipated and wished for.

At the next opportunity, together with his laptop, the aid of the company printer and a sheet of the hospital headed paper that Isabella had obtained, he devised an official-looking letter in English. Then with the second piece of headed paper, together with the aid of the laptop translation programme, he printed an identical letter in Spanish.

Following the completion of the tasks, Dutch then contacted American Airlines. He explained his medical emergency and the urgency that he travelled at the oncoming weekend. The member of the sales team offered a destination of either London Heathrow or Gatwick Airport. Without hesitation, Dutch secured a booking on a flight to Gatwick via Miami and Madrid. At the same time he was feeling apprehensive, as although this destination was essential to his plan, he was aware having carried out past extensive work at the airport. It was policed by the Sussex force, the same county in which he was possibly wanted. It was very probable that all of the officers stationed there would have been previously made aware of his suspected transgressions. At the request of the company ticketing office, he immediately emailed his self-composed hospital referral letters, receiving a prompt reply stating that he had been given special dispensation on the weekend flight due to his urgent medical appointment, and any assistance he required would be readily available throughout the journey.

Jose Enrique Zavala Hospital

Calle José Enrique Zavala, DeLauro 4118, Falcón, Venezuela
Sebastian Vasquez M.D
Ophthalmology Department
Tele 0410 5550376n.

To the Authority it may Concern

Today I preliminary examined the patient Mr Adam Stone, a forty-five-year-old American/ British citizen who is employed by Venouston Oil and Fuel Co. Mr Stone presented himself to the Emergency Department in extreme pain caused by an accident at his place of work at a nearby oil drilling plant, when a corrosive cleaning fluid containing lead methanol accidently came into contact with both eyes causing toxin amblyopia. I immediately bathed his eyes with an antibiotic eye solution and provided him with sedatives to ease the pain that he was experiencing. I observed that the flesh around his eye sockets was reddened and swollen. I suspect that there is a possibility of serious or permanent optic nerve damage to both eyes, but to establish the full extent of his injuries he would need to attend an ophthalmology department with the necessary specialist equipment.

During my examination, I received a telephone call from Mr Stone's employers in Houston, Texas, who were made aware of his predicament and have now received instructions from their insurers, that due to the possible serious consequences of this accident they wish Mr Stone to travel immediately to the London Eye Hospital, Harley Street, England, for further tests and treatment. I suggest that under these circumstances, he commence this journey as soon as possible. Dr Christopher Robson Smith, a consultant ophthalmic surgeon, will see Mr Stone as an emergency patient as soon as he arrives at his clinic. Mr Stone has been issued with sedatives and antibiotic eye solution sprays. I have suggested that he does not remove his dark glasses unless necessary to prevent foreign bodies entering the eyes and causing infection.

Copies of this letter together with my invoice have been forwarded to Venouston Oil and Fuels Company, Houston, Texas, for their information and the information of their insurers.

I wish Mr Stone a safe journey and a positive outcome.

Sebastian Vasquez M.D

Chapter 5
Running Blind (2004)

Artists: Godsmack
Writer: Salvatore P. Erna

With his departure plan assured, Dutch then told George and Bo of his immediate intentions. Like their new boss, they too suspected that he would soon follow his wife, so it was not a surprise to either of them. That evening all three of them, together with Holton, met in the small bar situated in the staff dining room of the compound reminiscing over Dutch's curtailed stay, with the three security members continually playing practical jokes and ribbing each other. Bo, whose real name was Cesar Rodriguez, gave a display of his singing and dancing ability, exhibiting why George had nicknamed him Bo due to his similarities to the character from the widely known popular song, Mr Bojangles. Claudia and Isabella, who provided food, also joined them, with Isabella having to leave early for her night shift at the hospital. Although, having only recently arrived, Holton was proving to be a pleasant and honourable boss, but Dutch was growing concerned as to his secluded lifestyle. His need as their boss required him to keep a certain distance between him and his workforce, which meant that at the end of the working day and on rest days he was alone. The only relief from his isolation was his regular use of the gym and swimming pool, with the occasional basketball shoot-out with George.

Although, a jovial experience, the evening proved somewhat emotional for the three men, who during Dutch's stay had worked closely together covering each other's backs in a hostile environment on almost a daily basis.

The night ended with George disappearing to his apartment with Claudia, and Bo having to sleep in Dutch's apartment as he had drunk too much, rendering him incapable of driving to his home.

As the team were not required to work on the Saturday of Dutch's departure, Holton gave authorisation for George to convey him to La Chamita Airport. In order to make his deceptive travelling plan appear realistic, Dutch only carried an aluminium flight case containing toiletries, clean underwear and socks together with his reflective works jacket. As his intended scheme required him to carry minimum luggage, he shared the property he had been forced to leave behind between George and Bo. These items included his personal laptop and mobile telephone, as he was conscious that if seized they could be subject to electronic interrogation. Amongst the property he carried on his person were the personal documents and passports once belonging to Adam Stone, letters purported to originate from DeLauro Hospital, a folding white walking cane, a pair of wraparound sunglasses, a bottle of hospital-issued eye spray and painkillers. Amongst the casual attire that he was wearing was the pair of running shorts with the pocket containing the neck ribbon and fake identification card. He was also now in possession of a large amount of US dollars, some of which were wages owed to him that Chamberlain had authorised to be paid from the White House safe, together with cash Dutch had saved during his stay. If questioned regarding the large amount of currency he carried, he would state that he had no idea how long his treatment would take, or if he would be required to pay for this treatment himself before being reimbursed by the company insurers.

During the time that George and Dutch had worked together, neither had confided in each other as to why they had entered Venezuela, one of the few countries in the world that either had no extradition agreement with other countries or did not always honour such agreements even when in place. They both suspected that each other were there to avoid a serious problem within their own country, but as neither of them was proud of their past actions, such a subject was never discussed.

Amongst their laughing and joking during the ninety-mile journey, they discussed as to how Holton would cope with the new lifestyle that he had entered into, and what Dutch's replacement would be like.

As the airport building came into sight, Dutch requested George to pull over into a secluded lay-by.

George did as was asked, quipping, "Man, you must be desperate for a piss, the bathroom in the airport is only a few minutes away."

"I don't need a piss, George. I've got something to tell you and I need your help."

"Oh boy. I knew you were up to something. I was wondering what you were up to as you have been very secretive lately. What's with the hospital papers and eye spray that Isabella got you, growing that beard and finding you stumbling around the car park with a stick wearing dark glasses? It's all seemed very weird."

"Okay, I will tell you straight. I can't get back to England on my passport as if I did I would be arrested for murder. I was hell-bent on revenge after the physical and mental torture that a gang inflicted on Melanie."

George did not look at all surprised, casually replying, "Sorry to hear that, Dutch. Knowing you as I do, I'm sure you were justified in whatever you did. We are virtually trapped here, just like many other non-Venezuelans in similar circumstances. In my case, it was me or the other guy and it wasn't going to be me, but the authorities wouldn't see it that way."

"If, like me, you can't return to your home country, what will you do when your time is up here?"

"Not entirely sure. As you know there is nothing to spend money on when stuck inside of that compound almost all of the time, so I have saved a lot of my pay and other extra income that you now know about. I doubt if I will stay in this country. Now I've had some experience with the launch at the island site I would like to think that I might buy a boat and travel a bit. Of course, wherever I go I will have to avoid the law."

"Sounds good. Taking either of the ladies with you?"

"Who knows? I may even take both."

"You alone with two women together in a confined space. You are a better man than me, George. Mind, there's enough of you to share around. You never know I may catch your next movie and unfortunately, because I couldn't look away in time, I will now recognise that it's you even if you don't show your face."

George laughingly replied, "You may mock but think about it. One is a cook and the other a housekeeper. All that is left for me to do is fishing and regular threesome sex sessions. What more could a man wish for."

"That would make life aboard very interesting, but I'm not sure how long those two would get on together under those circumstances."

"That's maybe, but when I do leave Venousten my options will be very limited."

"I guessed you had a similar problem, George, but I may have found a way out. As you know before I arrived here Rock Stone was kidnapped and later killed by a gang when it is suspected that they discovered he was the wrong person and not the boss who they wanted. I don't know if you knew, but according to Mr Chamberlain, Rock's ex-wife refused to accept his personal possessions and they remained in a drawer which is now in my room. There were only documents and his passports in there and…"

Before he could finish George said, "Man, you're going to use his passports aren't you? I wondered what that beard was all about."

"I've got to give it a go, George, as I think Melanie and her family may be in danger from some people I upset."

George said, "Let me have a look at the photos in those passports."

Dutch removed the passports from the plastic wallet containing his documents, which included Stone's medical insurance card and driving licence, and handed the passports to George.

Having opened the passports, George examined the image of Stone and glanced quickly at Dutch then saying, "With a quick look that's not bad, trouble is many of the airports have got facial recognition systems now. I know they haven't got it here yet, but what happens when you get to England, as I would imagine they have all the up-to-date technology?"

"You're right but I may have had an idea to get over that."

Following this remark, Dutch lifted his case from the back seat, opened it and removed the collapsible cane, sunglasses, eye spray and painkillers. He then produced the letters purporting to be from the hospital which he handed to George, who closely examined them both before saying in a bemused tone, "Man. You've got some nerve, so you are going to travel on Rock's passports, but why do you need to fake temporary loss of your eye sight?"

"This way I will hopefully get dispensation and get to keep the dark glasses on, which will help me get over the passport photo problem, but not sure how to deal with any facial recognition system. The fact that Rock has dual passports and was born in England will help with me not having an American accent. I have to get back whatever the outcome."

"What if they check with either doctor you've named on the letter?"

"That's why I am travelling on Saturday, I've checked and neither works at weekends."

"Man, that's genius! Do you know what the funny thing is, Dutch? I knew Rock's passports were there and I so wished that I could have used them. The trouble is he was about six inches shorter and half as wide, and white."

"Didn't really tick to many of the boxes did it?"

Both men burst out laughing.

George then said, "The likeness of you and that photo isn't bad, but he was far better looking than you, so you need to cover your face more." He then took off his black Atlanta Hawks' logoed basketball cap, placed it on Dutch's head and pulled it low over his eyes, at the same time adjusting it to size by the Velcro back strap.

Looking in the rear-view mirror, Dutch said, "Not a bad fit. I don't usually wear hats; do you think it will help?"

"Maybe not, buddy, but it will help stop you frightening the children with your ugly mug. It's also a small token to remember me by."

Dutch, with the knowledge that George was very fond of the headwear, and feeling quite emotional at his comment and gift, placed out his right hand in the direction of his colleague, who responded by participating in a lengthy hand shake. Dutch could see and sense the honesty and emotion in his friend's farewell gesture, which an outsider would not have associated with such a huge fearsome looking man. As they held their grip both men were aware that, even though now being good friends, due to their individual circumstances they would never meet again. Dutch then adjusted his newly acquired cap, added the sunglasses saying, "Now you know what I am up to, would you mind assisting this poor old injured soul to the check-in desk as my eyesight is shortly going to be impaired?"

They both chuckled at the comment.

"Of course, how could I let someone in such a predicament stumble across the concourse with only the aid of his stick? I shall lay it on so heavy for you with the ground staff they will tend to your every need, but don't get over-emotional about that gift of the cap. The Hawks are playing crap at the moment and are bottom of the standings, so I'm not feeling it at the moment."

Looking aghast and smiling, Dutch replied, "After all the time I've been here, I was just beginning to like you George, and now you go and ruin it."

George then drove into the airport complex, taking advantage of his seemingly disabled passenger by parking in a disabled marked bay close to the terminal building. George, continued to play his part well by quickly alighting from the vehicle and assisting his apparently partially sighted passenger onto the pavement, and he then retrieved his small case from the car. As George led him by the arm to the check-in desk, it was now the turn of Dutch to put his rehearsals to the test by holding his cane in a prominent position for all to see, taking short unsteady steps through the busy concourse. Once at the appropriate check-in desk and having made their introductions, George took the plastic wallet from Dutch, producing his tickets and the Spanish language hospital letter to the female assistant.

Hospital José Enrique Zavala

Calle José Enrique Zavala, De Lauro 4118, Falcón, Venezuela
Dr. Sebastián Vesque

Departamento de Oftalmología
Tele 0410 5550376.

A la autoridad correspondiente

Hoy he realizado un examen preliminar al paciente Sr. Adam Stone, un ciudadano estadounidense o británico de 45 años de edad, quien es empleado de Venouston Oil and Fuel Co. El Sr. Stone se presentó en el Departamento de Emergencias con un dolor extremo causado por un accidente en su lugar de trabajo en una planta de perforación petrolera cercana, cuando un líquido de limpieza corrosivo que contenía metanol con plomo accidentalmente entró en contacto con ambos ojos causando ambliopía toxica. Inmediatamente le lavé los ojos con una solución ocular con antibióticos y le proporcioné sedantes para aliviar el dolor que estaba experimentando. Observé que el tejido alrededor de sus órbitas oculares estaba enrojecido e hinchado. Sospecho que hay una posibilidad de daño serio o permanente del nervio óptico en ambos ojos, pero para establecerse la extensión completa de sus lesiones el paciente necesitaría asistir a un departamento de oftalmología con el equipo especializado necesario. Durante mi examen recibí una llamada telefónica de los patrones del Sr. Stone en Houston, Texas quienes habían sido informados de los hechos, ya han recibido instrucciones de sus aseguradores, que debido a las posibles serias consecuencias de este accidente desean que el Sr. Stone viaje inmediatamente al London Eye Hospital, Harley Street, Inglaterra para más pruebas y tratamiento. Sugiero que, dadas las circunstancias, inicie este viaje lo antes posible. El Dr. Christopher Robson Smith, un consultor cirujano oftálmico, vera al Sr. Stone como paciente de emergencia tan pronto como llegue a su clínica. Al Sr. Stone se le han suministrado sedantes y aerosoles de soluciones oculares antibióticas. He sugerido que no se quite sus anteojos oscuros, a menos que sea necesario para evitar que cuerpos extraños entren en sus ojos y provoquen una infección Copias de esta carta junto con mi factura han sido enviadas a Venouston Oil and Fuel Co. Houston, Texas para su información y la información de sus aseguradores.

Le deseo al Sr.Stone un viaje seguro y un resultadopositivo.

Dr Sebastián Vásquez

It became apparent to Dutch that his friend was enjoying every moment in his part of the deception and was doing a bloody good job at it, almost making Dutch feel that his vision was in fact impaired as he was having genuine problems seeing clearly through the very dark lenses. Having read the letter and scanned her computer records, the female ticket clerk, who spoke enough English to fully understand, asked Dutch in a very sympathetic manner the routine questions that all passengers faced. Also, she informed him that he was being provided with mobile assistance. This came as a shock to Dutch, as he had only envisaged a personal walking guide at the airports and now felt almost embarrassed, but his thoughts were that this introduction could only benefit the authenticity of his scheme. The acceptance that his flight case could travel with him as hand luggage was valuable news for Dutch, as the item could prove vital towards his intended deception.

As both men stood alone close to the desk waiting for the assistant, George in a quiet tone said, "How was my acting? I thought it was pretty darn cool."

"Possibly too good. I'm now going to be driven around in a disability carrier, which in some ways is perfect, but I will feel a right plonker. I suppose, that shouldn't bother me if it helps me get through this."

"I enjoyed that role and thought that I was pretty convincing. I always fancied myself as an actor."

"You were. I almost started to believe it myself."

Within a short time, a male attendant approached them pushing a wheelchair. Dutch, trying not to appear embarrassed, settled himself on the seat and both George and he quit their ribbing and said their sincere final farewells, with both men promising to stay in touch via Skype.

Before reaching passport control, Dutch requested his aide, in some of the few Spanish words he knew, to convey him to the toilets. Once there the attendant waited whilst Dutch unsteadily made his way inside, purposely exaggerating an unsteady gait by attentively tapping his stick from side to side as he went. After using the urinal and washing his hands, he then removed his sunglasses, placed an excessive amount of the eye solution in each eye causing the fluid to leave tracks down his cheeks. Making sure he was alone, he then looked into the fixed mirror, feeling satisfied with the distressed facial image that he had created.

On reaching passport control he handed over the passports once belonging to Stone. The official made a brief examination of the details and photographs inside. He then looked at Dutch, asking him to remove his sunglasses. Dutch tentatively removed them, at the same time closing his eyes and wincing as if the light was causing him pain. On seeing his discomfort, the official indicated for him to quickly put them back on saying, *"Cual es tu problema?"*

Dutch replied, "I only speak a little Spanish. If you are asking my problem, I accidently had methanol sprayed in my eyes."

The attendant, realising that the official did not speak English said, *"Fluido industrial en sus ojos."*

The official then ushered them through into the search area where with assistance. Dutch left his seat and removed his shoes, watch, and the contents of his pockets; and placed them together with his cane and case onto the screening belt. The attendant viewing the images informed Dutch that he would be permitted to carry his prescribed eye spray aboard his flight. He then walked through the metal scanning arch, feeling relieved that he had replaced the metal clasp that had previously attached the lanyard to the ID pouch, which was contained in the pocket of the shorts that he was wearing. Reunited with his helper, he was then pushed to the gate to wait for his departure to Miami feeling a great sense of relief that he had tackled the first hurdle of what he was sure were many more to come before he fully completed his task. After a long wait sitting alone, he finally heard his flight number called over the tannoy system and was shortly joined by a ground hostess. After a short conversation she guided him down a flight of concrete stairs and out of the terminal building onto the aircraft-parking bay and to the foot of the steps leading into the American airliner, where he was introduced to a waiting air hostess. The hostess then assisted Dutch up the stairs and into his allotted aisle seat. Due to his apparent injury, he was the first person to enter the aircraft. He was feeling pleased with his aisle seating position, since he would only have one person beside him who may attempt to make conversation, as he wished to avoid any questions about himself or his travel details. He would not be able to be truthful, and one lie would eventually lead to another, so he would be forced to feign sleep or appear to be standoffish.

Dutch had little worry about being bothered with conversation before the commencement of his twenty-two-hour long journey, as the middle-aged woman seated next to him was Spanish-speaking and spent almost the entire journey talking to her family in her native tongue.

The relatively short flight to Miami proved to be an extremely boring experience for Dutch, as a supposed traveller with serious eye injuries he could hardly be seen reading the in-flight magazine or watching the featured films. It was now that he began to realise how the circumstances he had created would make a lengthy trip seem like an eternity. He did, however, take the opportunity to mull over at length his two possible plans of action on reaching Gatwick Airport.

On his much-welcomed arrival at Miami, he was provided with the identical courtesy as at La Chinita. After disembarking, the ground hostess guided him along the piers into the terminal building, where he again boarded an awaiting similar wheelchair as he had previously experienced. Having passed through several official-looking areas, Dutch was informed by his carer that they had arrived at his required departure zone and was assisted to a seat in the waiting area. The choosing of this particular flight was relevant, even though the times between connections were lengthy, it did not require him to leave the terminal building at any time; allowing him to remain in a restricted airside area and rendering it unnecessary for him to be vetted again. While waiting for his connecting flight, Dutch took the opportunity to change some of his American currency into British pounds.

Following his flight to Spain, he was further pleased that exactly the same undemanding procedure occurred at Madrid Airport.

He was now on the final leg home with only a few hours to decide on which of his plans to implement. Plan A was to front it out and go through the entire airport exit procedure, in the hope that neither special branch officers nor patrolling police officers would recognise him from any previously circulated photographs. To succeed, this would also mean his disguise and paperwork would need to stand up to the test. He would also have to hope to avoid any facial recognition equipment. Plan B was entirely more unpredictable, as although he had some local knowledge from the past, he was aware that the circumstances and the procedures at such high-risk establishments could change very quickly.

Both options were very risky and if either failed he knew arrest was inevitable. One of his most important judgements, during two careers of making many life and death decisions, was soon to be made.

Dutch decided that as soon as the hostess announced that the pilot was preparing the final approach procedures for landing he would choose his plan of action. When the announcement came, after all of the hours of long drawn out considerations, he chose plan B. His final reasoning for this was that, even in the worst-case scenario at being discovered, he may have the chance to run and hide, an option that would not be available to him with plan A, inside a heavily populated airport building with an abundance of police and security staff. He felt a pang of satisfaction regarding his choice, when he learnt from a cabin announcement that the aircraft was disembarking at Gatwick South Terminal, which he considered would give his scheme a far greater chance of success.

Chapter 6
Going Underground (1980)

Artists: The Jam
Writer: Paul Weller

Once landed Dutch, with his heart now pounding in anticipation as to what lay ahead, located his case and stick in the overhead locker and shuffled in a line of fellow passengers towards the front of the aircraft, where the door was now connected to a pier by way of a stretch bridge. On reaching the hostess standing by the exit door, he was introduced to a member of the ground crew who guided him through the tunnel to an awaiting battery-operated buggy. Dutch then informed the attendant that he did not require the transport, as even with his limited sight he would be capable of making his own way through the wide and well-lit corridors unaided. He did, however, ask for directions to the nearest toilet, as he required the use of the facilities with some urgency.

After assuring the attendant of his capability and that he had a companion waiting to meet him, he was subsequently directed to a nearby toilet. Dutch then proceeded to maintain his facade to the toilet door, but once inside the deserted washroom and after removing his dark glasses he entered a cubicle, locking the door behind him. He then placed his case on the top of the toilet cistern and removed the reflective jacket from inside, placing it over his own jacket. After that he dismantled his walking cane, and he placed it in the case with his documents and the now redundant dark glasses. He closed the case, loosened his belt, placed his hand down his shorts and removed the identity card and neck ribbon from the inner pouch. After putting the ribbon over his head and around his neck, he adjusted his newly acquired gifted headwear. Dutch then decided to wait inside the cubicle to allow sufficient time for all the passengers and attendants associated with his flight to leave the immediate area. When certain that there was nobody else present in the washroom outside, he vacated the cubicle, immediately inspecting his image in the large glass mirror. Approving of what he saw he confidently exited the toilet, turned left down the aisle, returning towards the area where he had departed from the aircraft. He then descended a set of stairs that he had previously managed to see through the dark glasses, then walked from the pier onto the edge of the concrete aircraft parking bays. With a quick glance towards the aircraft on which he had arrived, he saw that the telescopic tunnel was still attached; therefore, he would not be visible to any remaining crew who may have possibly identified him. Although, it was early morning as usual at the busy airport; there were still numerous maintenance workers, tug drivers and baggage loaders in the area dressed similar to him, with some carrying tool boxes resembling his flight case.

For a second or two he remained stationary, scanning to his left in search of a specific area. As soon as the desired location came into his view, he started to walk to his destination between the pier and the various parked aircraft pushback tugs and the large mobile staircases.

On reaching the foot of the main terminal building, he could see black metal safety rails surrounding a concrete stairway. Prior to descending the steps, he perused the area to see if he had attracted any attention from anyone present. Satisfied that he was not being observed, he quickly walked down into the darkness, where he was confronted with a metal fire door. With some trepidation, he pushed down on the handle knowing that if the door was locked, he would be forced to revert to his less favourable plan A.

To his relief the door was not locked, as was always the case when he had worked here over two years ago maintaining and repairing the water supply that flowed through the numerous lengths of pipes underneath the original South Terminal building. His former boss and ex-army colleague Jon Shipway, the proprietor of Clearwater Revival, sub-contacted to Southern Waterways, who in turn had a contract with the Airports Authority. When several problems occurred with some of the water pumps beneath the building, Dutch had been dispatched there to replace some of the ageing pumps and pipes. He had spent an entire week in the labyrinth of the wide and well-lit tunnels. The roof space and either side of the warren of tunnels carried miles of pipes and cables of all the essential services, which meant there were always various personnel working there day and night. During his work there, it had been necessary for Dutch to enter and familiarise himself with most of the tunnels underneath the original terminal building, and being an inquisitive person he had explored the entire subterranean complex. To gain entry to the airport's secure areas it had been necessary for him to obtain both security passes for himself and the vehicle he was using at the time. He hoped that he had clearly remembered the details of the pass that had once been issued to him, further hoping that its format had not altered significantly, and still closely resembled his forgery.

Once through the door and into the tunnel, he was relieved to see the remaining piece required for his planned exit. Upon the wall were a row of hanging pegs on which hung both fluorescent waistcoats and jackets and various coloured plastic hard hats. These items were made readily available for any workers who had forgotten or lost their own, or for visitors of management level, as anyone not wearing either would be deemed to be contravening health and safety regulations and not permitted access to the tunnels. Dutch chose a yellow hard hat, with the knowledge that most of the companies employed there favoured that colour. He then swapped over his headwear, placing the now redundant baseball cap into his pocket. Dutch then walked from the entrance into the main service tunnel where he could hear voices echoing in the distance. At quiet times every noise and conversation were amplified throughout the passages. From parts of the conversation he could hear from those present, he was able to establish that the voices were that of male Telecom engineers. He then made his way to an alcove situated behind two large chrome boiler tanks close to the only landside exit. It was in this alcove that Dutch and his work colleague Zak regularly sat for their tea breaks, rather than wasting their rest time by leaving the area and walking to the staff canteen. He had previously decided that this is where he would pause until his best opportunity unfolded. As he waited for his moment, he knew exactly what he would do if successful, but must prepare for the worst-case scenario which was arrest. If this occurred, he could not be found in possession of either the documents or the passports issued to Stone, or anything appertaining to his deception, as such offences carried severe sentences. He thought how ironic it would be if the police had no evidence with regards to the five deaths that they suspected him of being responsible for, but instead he got banged up for contravening immigration laws.

In literally a flash, flames for the base of one of the boilers sprang into life and the roar of the intensity of the flames could be clearly heard. In an instant, Dutch knew this was the moment he had been waiting for. Firstly, he needed to destroy all of the incriminating items. He then began to quietly tear up the passports and documents, then, with his knowledge of such water boilers, he opened the service chamber and fed small amounts of the paper onto the gas supplied rack of intense flames. After each feed he would close the service hatch to initially prevent any excess smoke entering the tunnels and activating the smoke alarms. Once the papers were completely destroyed, he removed the dark glasses from his case and, together with the plastic container of eye drops, tossed them into the inferno, both of which immediately shrivelled into molten balls. It was now time for the final phase of his extraction plan. With some regret, he pulled George's gift from the pocket of the reflective jacket that he was wearing, with the knowledge that there would be no objection from the big man if he knew how crucial the sacrifice of the present was about to be. The forfeiture was made easier as George had temporarily lost faith in his favourite basketball team. Dutch then fully re-opened the hatch and by holding the peak of the cap placed it on the flames, allowing the smoke generated from the material to escape into the corridor, which he assisted by wafting the vapour with the vigorous waving of his arms. Dutch could clearly see the nearby fire alarm fitted in the roof of the corridor and awaited the inevitable.

After less than a minute, a deafening shrill-sounding alarm reverberated around the corridors. Dutch readied himself and carried out some quick deep breaths and leg stretches in anticipation of a possible need to sprint. From looking in between the two large water tanks he was able to observe the passageway that any evacuees would need to pass to reach the landside exit door. As soon as three men dressed identical to himself walked noisily into his sight, he sprang out from the alcove and followed unnoticed in the heels of the last man. As they all strode towards the exit, Dutch was prepared to be confronted by one of the ever-present security officers stationed at the entrance and exit point. It was general practice among the various security officers to carefully scrutinise the passes of the workers entering the tunnels, but they were not so vigilant to those exiting and Dutch was hoping this practice still applied. A guard was usually positioned at the door at the top of the steps, but due to the alarm, the officer was standing at the foot of the stairs indicating for the group of four to hurry. On reaching the guard who was holding a walkie-talkie to his ear and standing immediately underneath a whirring and flashing red warning light, the three men in front of Dutch automatically produced their security passes from under their jackets, quickly flashing them in the guard's direction. Dutch was quick to do the same, but the guard was taking little notice of the group of four or their passes as he was more intent at peering down the tunnel, at the same time as talking on his radio. Due to the intense sound of both the rotating red light and the alarms, the guard was forced to shout to the lead worker asking him if they had in any way set the alarms off, or if they had seen any sign of fire. He was given a negative result to both questions, and when then asked if their workforce was all accounted for the first man, looking at his two colleagues, confirmed that they were. It was then suggested that they take the exit stairs and wait outside until the tunnels had been inspected by the fire service which had been automatically been alerted. The three workers, together with Dutch, then started to ascend the concrete staircase, giving the guard the impression that all four men were from the same company.

Throughout their short and loud conversation, if it had proved necessary, Dutch was alert and ready to push past the three men, run up the steps and across the road where he would be confronted with only a six-foot wire mesh fence in the less secure landside area. He thought that with the surprise advantage, together with the confusion of the fire alert, he would have sufficient time to scale the fence before the guard emerged from the tunnel. This would also allow him time to throw both his hard hat and case over the fence before him, as his fingerprints and DNA would be present on each item. As he moved up the stairwell Dutch was half expecting a call from the guard to return, so was mighty relieved as he exited into the daylight. Once out of one tunnel system they all emerged into another tunnel. This tunnel was open and much larger, with a wide service road which carried only authorised airport traffic under the South Terminal building. The three telecommunication workers waited and chatted by the exit door, not giving Dutch a second glance as he started to walk through the tunnel, which accentuated the deafening sound of the sirens of the arriving fire engines. He was not surprised at the swift attendance of both airport and county fire services, as such a building would be treated as a high-risk priority. At that time there were few people present in the area, but those there were watching the firefighters, and took no notice at all of a man striding out of the tunnel dressed in working attire.

Emerging from the tunnel, Dutch crossed the service road and made the short walk to the pavement of the A23 London to Brighton trunk road which he also crossed. He then located and walked along the tree-lined cycle and Pedestrian Avenue that led from the terminal building under yet another tunnel, which burrowed beneath the M23 spur road leading into the nearby town of Horley. Although, tired after his long and cramped journey, he enjoyed stretching his legs on the twenty-minute walk to the town's railway station, which provided a direct service to his destination of Brighton. At times he felt the impulse to run on the open paths and pavements, as he had not been afforded the opportunity to run freely outside of his Venezuelan accommodation for almost two years. He would have broken into a jog had he not been wearing a safety hard hat, reflective waistcoat and carrying a small case; he considered doing so would attract attention that he did not desire.

Arriving at the rail station, he purchased a one-way ticket to Brighton. Being early Sunday morning meant a restricted weekend service which caused him to endure a lengthy wait. Nonetheless, despite sitting on a hard-uncomfortable metal bench in the cold and drizzling rain, and regardless of the enormous problems he was soon to face, he felt home again. This was his country and he didn't wish to be anywhere else in the world. From that moment he vowed that whatever the future was to bring, he would never leave British shores again. Once aboard the train he began to realise how much he had missed the prominently green Sussex countryside. When the train stopped at Hassocks, he took note of all the surroundings both in and around the station, as he suspected that he may well be returning to the location in the near future.

On his arrival in Brighton, now carrying his hard hat and reflective jacket, he made his way to a small back street café that was popular with the local manual workers and which had a reputation for producing a fine early morning full

English breakfast. Even though it was Sunday morning, the café was open and many of the tables were taken by the diners; not all workmen as some had obviously made it their first stop after leaving the local late-night clubs or parties. Before taking a seat, he hung his hat and jacket that he had been carrying on the rack provided. Dutch was not a regular fried breakfast eater, as he tried to keep to a good balanced diet, but this was a treat that he just could not miss. Little of the food supplied in Venezuela, except for the fruit, had been to his taste. He was now especially looking forward to some traditional fried egg, bacon, beans and sausages, accompanied by a mug of tea, so from the menu he ordered 'The Full Monty'. While waiting for his meal to arrive he picked up a two-day old copy of the local newspaper, 'The Evening Argus', and was not surprised to read that crime and drugs were still very prominent in the city.

Having consumed a very large enjoyable meal, which despite its unhealthy reputation had very much lived up to his expectations, he was now beginning to feel the effects of his long journey but had some purchases to make before he could sleep. After paying for his meal, he left the premises deliberately leaving the hat and jacket on the pegs, as they had now served his purpose and which would also now be readily available to aid a future customer who may require either item. His next port of call was a small mobile telephone shop in the city centre which he had dealt with before and found very helpful. Here he purchased two pay-as-you-go mobile telephones, each of a different brand and distinguishable not only by sight but also by feel, as would be imperative for to him to recognise each even in darkness. He paid cash and remained anonymous throughout the transaction in order that the telephones could not be traced to him. His final purchase that morning was a pair of 'off the shelf' reading spectacles. On his way to the bus stop servicing the Kemptown area of the city, he saw an assortment of gifted items which had been left in the doorway of a closed charity shop. Dutch then took the opportunity to dispose of another redundant piece of his past deception. He opened his case, and took out the retracted walking cane, placing it amongst the donations.

Just prior to his sister Jeanette answering the door to him at her home in Chapel Street, in the Kemptown area, on the edge of the city centre; Dutch was reminded of both happy and sad times that he had shared when he and his brother and sisters lived there with his grandparents. Following the death of Connie and then Sinbad, Jeanette had taken over the tenancy. On seeing Dutch she initially examined him quizzically, when after a few seconds, he was met with a loud scream of surprise followed by, "Dennis, it's you. I can't believe it. Come in. I hardly recognised you with that beard and longer hair."

Dutch, having looked around the street, and pleased that it seemed that nobody had been alerted to her shriek, smiled replying, "Yes, it is really me, Sis. I'm glad you didn't immediately recognise me, if my own sister is not sure, that gives me some hope of nobody else doing so. No more screaming like that though, I'm trying to keep a low profile."

"I'm sorry about that, but you were the last person I expected to see, especially as your passport and papers arrived here yesterday with little explanation, so I couldn't imagine how you could possibly get back. Mind you, when Melanie phoned to say that she had returned I suspected that you wouldn't be far behind. Wild horses wouldn't keep you two apart for long."

"For various reasons I needed to get back here, but that's a story for another day. How are you and Martin doing?"

"That's all over. He's buggered off, gone back to live with his parents. No problems though, we just weren't getting on."

"Sorry to hear that, Sis, but if it wasn't working then for the best I suppose."

"Don't worry I'm over it now. I've just started seeing someone else."

"You don't hang about, do you? Does he know about me?"

86

"Oh yeah, what a great chat-up line that would be: by the way, my brother is wanted for killing five men. Of course, I haven't, you dickhead. I'm presuming by the way you are talking that the police still want to talk to you. They came here several times asking questions shortly after you left."

"They will definitely still want to see me, and as I haven't got a clue what will happen after. I need to avoid them until I have sorted something out. Until I do, Melanie or her parents may be in danger."

"Oh no, not more problems for Melanie. You two have had more than your share over the years."

"Yes, unfortunately some of my instinctive actions haven't helped matters, but I can't go back on that now."

"I won't ask you all about that as I'm sure that you had your reasons. You look knackered. Do you want anything to eat or drink?"

"No. I don't want to appear rude, but I need to get some sleep and get myself organised, as I expect to have some long days and nights ahead. Apart from the passport, has a parcel arrived?"

"Yes, something arrived by courier. I'll get them both."

Jeanette then left the room, returning with the jiffy bag that he had dispatched containing his passport and papers, together with a medium-sized parcel. Inside the parcel wrapping was a box which Dutch opened. After removing the contents, he examined four metal stick-like objects contained inside.

Jeanette said, "What on earth are those things?"

"These are ground movement detectors, commonly known as tremble sticks. Every home should have some around their property, especially at night, as they can act as an alarm. The only drawback is they need to be monitored by a transistor radio and I haven't got one at the moment."

"Dennis, that's the worst hint I have ever heard. Why don't you just ask me if I've got one?"

"I didn't want to ask as I have more favours to ask, yet."

"I will help my brother anyway I can. I will just pop out and get the radio that Martin's left in the shed."

On Jeanette's return, he tested the monitors with the small battery-operated radio and found each one was working perfectly.

"Do I dare ask what you want them for?"

"Best you don't know. If Martin comes back for it, tell him that I will return the radio, hopefully very soon. By the way do you still do a bit of hairdressing?"

"Why, do you want me to cut it for you, its longer than you usually have it?"

"Not yet, Sis, but soon. When I have finished what I need to do, I will need a place to stay. Would you mind if I stay here for a short time? I promise that I won't bring any trouble to your door?"

"Yes, of course, you can. You know that I have always kept a spare room ready in case of surprise visitors."

"Thanks, Jeanie, you're a star. Would you mind minding the passport and papers for me as I can't chance having them found on me, or I could end up in a police station before I'm ready? Thanks for everything, Jeanie but I must shoot off now as I have loads to sort out."

He then placed the detectors and radio in his case, kissed his sister on the cheek and made his way back to the bus stop.

On arriving in Woodingdean, to avoid being seen in Cowley Drive, Dutch entered his in-laws' property by walking through the fields on the well-used public footpath situated close to the rear of their bungalow.

He retrieved the keys to both the bungalow and the garage from the designated hide under a plant pot situated in the back garden. From the base of the nearby ornamental fountain, he carefully selected nine, being his lucky number, perfectly rounded beach pebbles. Despite feeling extremely tired, after only broken bouts of sleep during his long journey, he decided to prepare all that he required for the following day. Inside the garage, where much of Melanie's and his property had been stored since moving from their flat, there were large cardboard wardrobes and boxes, some of which contained many mementos and kit of his past military career, much of which he had not been required to return as the items had been personal issue or superseded by more recent models. From the labelled boxes he removed a large 100-litre Bergen rucksack, waterproof poncho, sleeping bag, and small shovel and pick axe, nylon ski mask, day and night time monocular sight, two metal mess tins, mug and cutlery and a small pocket torch which he was immediately able to load with new batteries. From another box he located a black cotton beanie hat which he placed to one side. After gathering all the retrieved property that he required, he packed the Bergen in military style order. On locating his father-in-law's fishing catapult, he placed it, together with the pebbles, in a side pocket of the rucksack. Once satisfied that he had all that he required, he locked the garage and entered the unoccupied bungalow relishing the thought of sleep. It was now late Sunday afternoon as he entered the spare bedroom now being temporarily used by Melanie, which was once her permanent place of sleeping until their marriage. As he settled between the cold sheets with the scent of his wife on the pillow, he felt both sad and responsible for the predicament he had placed her and her parents in. As he closed his eyes, he hoped that he would enjoy a long restful sleep in preparation for the anticipated long uncomfortable days and nights ahead.

When he awoke in the early hours, he felt fully refreshed. With time to kill, and with the thought of not being able to wash for several days, he relaxed in a long steaming bath, rehearsing what he was soon to say in a number of phone calls. With this in mind he made sure that both telephones had been fully charged overnight.

After foraging in the fridge and freezer, he ate a large breakfast in preparation for a far more meagre existence that lay ahead. Following the meal, he resumed his preparations by dressing entirely in warm dark practical clothing suitable for the environment in which he was to stay.

At 7:00 a.m. on the dot, from the specifically nominated mobile phone, he dialled the mobile number of Clearwater Revival, a name he had suggested for the company owned by his former boss and best friend Jon Shipway, once known as 'Jon The Pole' due to his outstanding athletic ability as a pole-vaulter. His call was answered immediately in a friendly efficient manner by a voice he clearly recognised and was pleased to hear.

"Good morning, Clearwater Revival. Jon speaking, how may I help?"

Dutch replied, "Ah! Jon of Clearwater Revival, then you must be the famous John Fogerty?"

His question prompted a few seconds of silence before Jon said, "Dutch, is that you?"

"How did you guess?"

"Because you are the only silly bugger I know who would piss about connecting Fogarty to my business."

"Nice of you to ask how I am, Jon. I'm very well, thanks. How are you?"

"Sorry, mate, but this is a bit of a surprise. I've been wondering how you were doing, as I hadn't heard anything since the messages we exchanged shortly after you left."

"There was a reason for that. At that time, I was never confident that any of my communications were not being monitored. You've obviously worked out what I was supposed to have done after you got a visit from the police and later from those two mobsters."

"Yeah, of course, but we better discuss that face to face. Where are you now, your voice is very clear, are you back?"

"We should be safe to talk on this phone, but I will tell you all when we next meet, which I hope will be very soon. To cut to the chase, Melanie could be in trouble, probably from those two geezers who visited you. I need to do something quickly and I have an idea, but I need a bit of help from you."

"Poor, Melanie. What with one thing and another, she's had some crap to deal with over the years."

"My impulsive actions haven't exactly helped, I know."

"What do you need me to do? I've helped you before, even though I had no idea what you were up to."

"I apologise for that, but that was because I didn't want to directly involve you or your company. When I tell you the whole story, you are one of the few people who will understand."

"Maybe. How can I help you both without getting myself banged up?"

"I'm not going to tell you anything for the same reason as before. I just want some information and a lift later, if that's possible?"

"Bloody hell, Dutch, you lead a complicated life. Fire away then."

"Did those Ferguson brothers who live in Albourne ever pay you for the work we did on their lake?"

"No. Don't get me talking about those two fuckers. It makes me mad just thinking about them, they owe me thousands."

"What! I knew that they owed you money but how come you haven't got it yet?"

"As you well know they were right rough London villains who moved there to get away from the heat of rival gangs and the law, supposedly to open a carp fishery. They contacted me about replacing pipes to the natural water supply for their lake. I gave them a price for the job and they paid me cash up front for the materials, so I thought all was okay, despite their widely known gruesome reputation. You worked on the job, met them and know how much work we put in there, but when I sent them the invoice for the labour for a perfectly completed job, I heard nothing back. I still had to pay the wages of the workforce so I phoned them time and time again and got nothing but excuses. When I paid them a visit to attempt to collect the payment, it was then I saw what vicious fuckers they could possibly be. They downright refused to pay anything, saying that our work was crap and was only worth the money they paid as a deposit, threatening that if I didn't fuck off of their property, they would shoot me there and then. When I got a bit verbal with them, the one you named Crank tore up their copy of the invoice in front of me, then picked up a piece of scaffold pole and threatened to wrap it around my head. I only had young Phil with me, I couldn't expect him to get involved, and so I had to back off. If you had been with me rather than jaunting off on a jolly to South America, we could have taken them on. So, I had to leave without the payment, but don't worry when I'm ready I have some ideas up my sleeve which should result in them taking an enforced vacation."

"Bastards. That's also made me angry. We all put a lot of hard graft in there and there was nothing wrong with the job. It was perfect."

"Exactly. I asked them what was wrong with the job and they couldn't give me an answer. They never ever intended to pay for the entire work. They paid that deposit to hook me in, and I fell for it. I distrusted them right from the start, as I can remember checking the notes that they gave me in case they were forgeries. I should have gone with my first gut instincts when they first contacted me."

"Does your future intended plan of revenge include informing the law as to what we thought was buried there?"

"Yeah, exactly that. I know someone who mixes in their dodgy circles. They apparently think that by living here, they are managing to operate under the police radar, so if I hear of any jobs that they are involved in I will bubble them up. It's not my usual practice on informing on anyone, not even those two shits, but they've pushed their luck too far and for too long this time. I did consider paying them a visit with some of the boys, but it would have only turned into a war. I probably wouldn't have got any money out of them anyway and the company name would be dragged through the mud. There's not much more that I can do as it's viewed as a civil matter. I have got to be a bit careful how I handle this one, as if I fail to get them nailed good and proper, if they thought I was responsible for informing the law they would probably torch my business."

"I doubt if they would especially think of you, as I'm sure that there are plenty queuing up to see them sent down. Anyway, hold those plans, buddy, as I have my own idea which should kill two birds with one, or more stones. I will say no more. All I need from you, Jon, is any telephone numbers you still have for them. Also, if I give you a call later, could you pick me up soon after from Brighton, and could you come in your car not a van?"

"I should be able to do that. Getting a bit fussy about what transport you use then? You were once as happy as a pig in shit when driving my vans. Have you been travelling around in limos or something?"

"Certainly, better standard wagons than you provided. I just need you and the car to give a particular impression."

"You cheeky bleeder. You disrespect my vehicles, then expect me to be your personal chauffeur."

"Only joking, mate. You know how I appreciated working for you and the use of that van. This is just the start of what I need to do to sort them and others out."

"I will be chuffed if we can get one over on those wankers. I will look through the files and give you a call back. I've resigned myself to losing the money, but some revenge would be nice, but with your reputation I'm not sure I like your reference to the killing of birds. I'm in the office all day so I can do the lift. I suppose it will be good to see you."

"The pleasure will be all yours. Give me a call back on this number. If things work out and I do call you later, you needn't say anything, just remember the address from where you need to pick me up, which I'm sure you've been to before. I'm pleased you never tackled them because when I was moving around their grounds digging in those pipes, the brother I nicknamed Popeye, as apparently he lost an eye in a stabbing incident, followed me everywhere. He told me where I could and couldn't dig. As you know it was obvious that they had dodgy gear, possibly even shooters buried there, so they're not to be messed with. Popeye looks the more intimidating, with his bulky body and one menacing eye, but believe me that Crank could be an evil, vicious bastard. As far as taking them on goes you are forgetting that we are both past our sell-by date."

"You speak for yourself. While you've been sunning yourself overseas, I've been keeping in shape by slaving away over a hot shovel."

"That's because you lost your best worker. Speak later, mucker."

"Yeah. See you shortly."

"I've told you before, don't call me shorty."

"I'm not sure what's worse, your so-called jokes or your bloody awful singing."

Dutch then terminated the call and waited for the necessary information from Jon.

In only a short time, he received the full address and telephone numbers that he required, and he in turn informed Jon of the location where he wished to meet him. The information he had received prompted him to locate the keys for Melanie's small Fiat that was parked in a neighbouring close and drive to the nearby Brighton Marina. After parking in the multi-storey car park of the large leisure complex, Dutch started to purchase essential shopping requirements from the large on-site supermarket. The majority of his shopping consisted of carefully selected chilled and easy cook meals, together with two, two litre bottles of water, toilet wipes, disposable plastic gloves and a radio hook-over earpiece.

Having put his newly acquired goods in the Fiat, he took a slow stroll along the Marina wall, looking out to sea; at the same time, appreciating what he felt he had missed while away from the shores of his beloved country for which he had fought and risked his life. When he reached the furthest point on the wall where the public were permitted, and having run through in his head some well-rehearsed lines, he sat down on a bench. Once he was certain that there was no one within hearing distance, he dialled the number that Jon had relayed to him on the second newly acquired phone, which because of its intended use and disposal, was commonly referred to as a 'Burnaphone'. Such named phones were for making and receiving spurious calls that could not connect the user to any phones possessed by other parties with whom it had contact, and this is exactly what he required it for.

His call was answered by a gruff male voice in a hostile manner:

"Who's that?"

Dutch spoke in what he considered was an equally forceful tone.

"You don't know me, but it will be of interest to both you and your brother if you listen to what I have to say."

Before Dutch could continue, with a raised and angry voice the recipient interrupted.

"Look here if you're trying to sell me something you can fuck off, and if you call again, I'll cut your balls off."

"No wait, don't put the phone down. I'm being serious here, someone's out to rob the both of you."

The voice on the other end of the phone sniggered, "Oh yeah, and who's got the balls to do that. You, you little prick?"

"No, not me, but I know about some heavy dudes who are planning to."

"Why are you telling me this? What's in it for you? You'll get fuck all from us."

"Revenge, that's all I want. I hate the bastards, I took the rap for them, and with a promise they would sort me out when I got out. You can guess the rest."

"How the fuck would you know this if you're not tied up with them?"

"Because their driver for the job is getting cold feet now, he knows of your reps, so he asked me how he could bottle it. I told him he couldn't back down now, they've given him the full SP. They wouldn't just let him walk. They are all tooled up, really evil Eastern European fuckers. They reckon that you've got decent gear hidden in your gaff and in the grounds. They are even bringing some nasty little devices to persuade you to tell them where you've stashed it."

This statement was met with a few seconds of complete silence, as if the phone had been temporarily muted. Dutch was certain that he had touched a nerve and the individual, having realised that there was possibly some credibility in the call, was possibly putting him on loudspeaker mode for his brother to also listen to the conversation.

"How do we know that you're not the filth setting us up for something? The bastards would love to cage us with a large one."

"Fair comment. You don't know for sure, but if the 'Feds' got caught setting you up this way they would be well in the shit."

"Let's say you're pukka. When is this supposed to kick off?"

"At night and very soon. So, if I were you, I would be ready twenty-four seven. Believe me they won't fuck around, apparently they've got active military experience. I hate these fuckers so much for the five I did for fuck all. I will be honest with you, that's not the only reason I'm warning you. Hopefully, you will be ready to sort them out, leaving a gap in the market for my business."

"How many handed is this crew then?"

"As far as I know just two, plus the driver who will be waiting for the off when they're done. I think from what he said it's probably a night time job, so I will know when, as he won't be in the pub that night. To give you a sporting chance I might even give you the heads up."

"You do that. How the fuck did you get this number anyway?"

"Carp fishery and Albourne was mentioned, so I didn't need any help from 'Nipper' of the yard. I became quite interested in you two, did a bit of surfing and saw that you both have been a bit lively over the years. You must be familiar with this sort of shit, so should be fuck all for you to sort out."

"It will be you getting sorted if we find you're fucking us about."

"I can understand why you might think I'm talking a load of crap, but there is no point in me pulling your plonker. If it does kick off, I suggest that you take no prisoners, cause believe me they will be back. They are determined fuckers."

Feeling fairly satisfied with his portrayal, Dutch terminated the call, at the same time ensuring that he switched the device off.

Following the call, he made a hurried return to the bungalow to prepare for the next phase of his intricate plan. Having dressed in his dark warm clothing, socks and boots; he felt far too warm for the weather conditions on such a mild day. Although, efficiently packed, he was forced to wear most of his clothing, as he was unable to fit anything further into his bulging rucksack which now contained all the items retrieved from the garage, together with the newly acquired foodstuffs and water bottles.

As midday approached, Dutch placed the beanie hat on his head, put on his reading glasses then inspected himself in a mirror. He was satisfied that the image he had now created with longer hair, beard, spectacles and hat was so distinctively different to his normal favoured look, he would hardly be recognisable as the same person. He then sat in a concealed position close to the front room window, constantly observing the driveway of the home of the man Melanie had dubbed Rab C. Nesbitt.

Chapter 7
Two Tribes Go to War (1984)

Artists: Frankie Goes to Hollywood
Writers: Gill, Johnson, O'Toole

A few minutes after midday, as Dutch sat sweating in his warm clothing, observing from behind the net curtains, he saw the man that Melanie had described as Rab C. Nesbitt walk down the path opposite him towards the road. Dutch couldn't help smiling to himself as to how his wife had so accurately described the man, similar to his own habit of giving nicknames to some individuals' characteristics. He then hurried to the front door and once outside slammed it hard shut, at the same time looking at the closed-door shouting, "That's it. I can't stay here a minute longer." He strode purposely towards the road with a grimace on his face. This had all been observed by Don McKinnon, who was slowly walking on the opposite pavement, taking a great deal of interest in Dutch's noisy exit from the bungalow.

As Dutch slammed the front garden metal gate, he called over to the pedestrian opposite, "Excuse me, mate. You don't know the phone number of a local cab company, do you?"

McKinnon turned to him and in slurred inebriated speech said, "Yeah I do. I don't drive anymore so use the cabs quite often." He then pulled a well-worn wallet from his pocket and started to sort through various business cards.

As Dutch approached, still fumbling through his wallet McKinnon said, "I haven't seen you about here before, just moved in?"

"I've been away, only got back recently and fallen out with that lot already. Anyway, I'm off on my own. I have managed to rent a cottage for a few days until I can sort things out. I haven't got a motor and neither of them will give me a lift. I wouldn't want them to at the moment anyway. We all need time apart to sort this mess out."

McKinnon selected a card and handed it towards Dutch who said, "I can't read small print very well even with these poxy specs. Could you read the number to me?"

Dutch carefully selected the chosen phone from his pocket, reduced the volume and held it at such an angle that McKinnon could not see the keypad. As McKinnon, with some difficulty slowly read the number from the card, Dutch could detect the strong smell of stale alcohol on his breath, whilst he mimicked pressing the dictated numbers but in fact speed dialled Jon, who answered immediately.

Dutch said with conviction, "Can I get a cab from Cowley Drive, Woodingdean to Lakeside Cottage, Birchwood Road, and Albourne in about forty-five minutes as I can't get the keys to the place before one o'clock."

Jon, guessing from the manner in which Dutch was talking that someone was close to him, said in a quiet tone, "Fuck me, Dutch, you said it was just as well I didn't tackle them, now you are about to do the same. You silly bastard."

Dutch, ignoring Jon's comment, paused as if the recipient was asking him for confirmation, and then said, "No, not quite right. Let me repeat the address, Lakeside Cottage, it's a cottage for rent at a carp fishery in Birchwood Road, Albourne."

Dutch paused again, then said, "No I won't have a load of fishing tackle, and I'm just renting the place alone for a couple of days as emergency accommodation."

Another pause then Dutch said, "Thank you," and ended the call.

McKinnon was standing close by throughout the whole conversation and Dutch made certain that he heard every word that he said.

Dutch then said, "Thanks for that. Once I've got the rest of my stuff I'm sorted."

McKinnon, placing the card back inside his wallet replied, "No problems pal. I've just got to pop back inside. I've forgotten something."

As McKinnon walked back towards his home, Dutch hoped that he was actually going to make a telephone call of what he had just overheard to a possible interested party. If his hunch was correct; although, he wasn't planning on going fishing, he may have just baited the hook. Just like the fisherman his late grandfather was, he now knew he was playing a waiting game.

Dutch watched McKinnon disappear into his overgrown garden and once he heard his door shut, he quickly re-entered his in-laws' bungalow, placing his fully laden rucksack just inside the front door ready for his exit. He then took up his concealed observation position at the front window and some ten minutes later saw McKinnon walk from his premises, continuing his previously intended journey. Not long after, as Melanie had predicted, he returned to his home carrying a plastic carrier bag which, by its shape, obviously contained more than one bottle.

With excellent timing Dutch saw Jon drive slowly by, at the same time pressing his horn to announce his arrival. As Jon carried out a three-point turn in the road, Dutch watched for any movement from the bungalow opposite and was pleased to see the curtains move slightly and Nesbitt peering out through the gap. After checking that he was leaving the bungalow tidy and fully secure, Dutch then replaced the hat and glasses, threw his rucksack over his shoulder, slammed the front door and again walked to Jon's car in an angry manner. On opening the rear door, he threw his luggage onto the seat, followed by himself.

On looking around at him Jon said, "Christ, Dutch, what the fuck's wrong with you? You look really pissed off. That's supposing that is you under that hair, beard, glasses and hat."

"Sorry, mate, it's just a temporary façade that I needed to perform as I am certain that I'm being watched, and if it comes down to it, I don't want to be recognised in the future. If you can drive towards Albourne I will explain on the way."

"By Christ you've got some explaining to do, that's for sure."

As they travelled on the twenty-minute journey, Dutch told his trusted friend why and how he had killed the five men involved in the rape, assault, filming and viewing of Melanie's horrendous ordeal. As much as Jon knew his friend, he found it difficult to believe how much meticulous planning and avoidance of any forensic evidence he had achieved so far. However, he was not surprised as to his drastic actions as Dutch had never been a man to be messed with, especially when it came to the protection of his wife, who had already had plenty of grief to contend with before the attack.

Following his explanation Jon asked, "You obviously can't run for ever. What have the police got on you?"

"As far as I know, only that my shoe size is the same as one found at a scene. Which proves nothing, but they may have gathered more while I've been away. I don't know."

"So not satisfied with what's gone before and all the serious shit you could be in, you are now planning another battle at forty-four years of age?"

"Believe me, Jon, if I could swerve this I would, but nobody but myself can get me out of this particular number. I doubt if the police will be particularly interested in my problem, which leaves Melanie wide open for any revenge they might take if I'm inside. You've seen the blokes looking for me. Be honest Jon, are they the sort who will just forget how I fucked up part of their organisation?"

"No, they are definitely not. They gave me the impression of being part of a really efficient, determined and nasty outfit."

"Well there you go. I have no choice, but hey ho, don't worry, this time I don't plan on my size nines even touching the ground near any of the action. Anyway, if it all goes to plan, I'm hoping that you too will get some satisfaction as to the outcome."

"If it doesn't, I may have a eulogy or some prison visiting requests to write."

"That's you, Jon, always the optimistic one. I won't tell you anymore, as like before the less you know the less involved you will be if it all goes bent."

"I feel that I should be involved with this one. After all, those two brothers ripped me off for thousands, for the unpaid work. I could easily make some arrangements and join you. It would be like old times."

"Sorry, mate, but no. For one thing I haven't got nearly enough equipment or food for two. You have already played a major part in my plot by being a supposed taxi. If I had walked or got the bus, the fella over the road would not have witnessed my departure which is essential to the plan. Also, I can't afford to be seen in such a remote location as people remember things like that. All I ask is that you don't mention this conversation or this journey to anyone, and if I am here longer than I expect could you ferry out some essentials to me?"

"You know that both of those go without saying. If I do have to come out to you, I'm getting involved, whatever you say. We are getting close now. If you are intent on going it alone, where do you want dropping?"

"Nowhere near their address, as some of the properties around there may have CCTV covering their entrances, including parts of the road. If you turn right when we get to that thatched restaurant at the next junction, I'm sure there will be a spot where I can get out and walk there through the woods."

"Before you do this, how sure are you that if whatever you're up to is successful and investigated by the police, that they won't make the connection that you once worked there?"

"I see no reason why work done two years ago should come to their notice, especially as you said that they had torn your invoice up."

"Fair enough, see you later. Be lucky."

"I will need it as I have run out of lives."

"Not that old chestnut again. You still believing in that crap."

"By believing, I once had nine lives, I always felt invincible. Now, I feel I may be vulnerable, but I don't plan on putting myself to the test any time soon."

Soon after making the turn, Dutch directed Jon to park in a small dirt pull-in on the nearside of the minor road. Not wishing them to be seen by any passing traffic, Dutch swiftly alighted from the car, and said a quick goodbye before disappearing into the trees and bushes carrying his heavy rucksack.

Before departing, and while attempting to view his friend manoeuvring through the densely wooded area, Jon so wished he had been in a position to join him in his quest. Not only for revenge on the two brothers, but also to help to free Dutch and Melanie from their precarious situation. In addition, he felt that 'digging in' and roughing it for a while would bring back valued memories of past times together in the military.

Once out of sight from the road, Dutch slung the straps of his rucksack over his shoulders. Feeling the heavy weight of the load reminded him of the numerous manoeuvres that he had been engaged in, when crossing miles of inhospitable barren landscape with similarly heavy bergens. With the aid of Ken's ordnance survey map, he commenced the one-and-a-half-mile trek to his planned destination. As he strode through the woods on the fine summer's afternoon, he noticed the spectacular beams of sunlight penetrating through the blankets of leaves on all the various species of trees; giving him the realisation that this was just another aspect of British life that he had missed and would never take for granted.

As he approached the end of the wooded area, it was now necessary for him to cross large open fields containing cattle, where he would be most vulnerable to human eyes. To prevent anyone taking an interest in his movements, rather than take shortcuts he again consulted the map following different sections of public bridleways and footpaths leading to his destination. As he walked the final section of footpath, he pushed himself through a less dense piece of hedgerow entering the woodland surrounding the lake owned by the Fergusons. Dutch walked parallel to the side of the lake, keeping well into the tree line as their cottage was now coming into his view. Just prior to the northern end of the lake, Dutch ascended a short steep wooded hill that overlooked both the lake and the house occupied by both brothers. From the summit he was able to survey the familiar scene below of which, due to his previous time working there, his knowledge of the lie of the land was better than most. By stooping low behind small saplings, he could see that very little had changed around the property since his last visit. On the one side of the lake, where fishing was permitted, there was a boathouse containing a small rowing boat and a number of wooden pontoons designating the various 'swims'. At that time, there were just two anglers fishing separately on the far side of the lake from his position, with their vehicles parked nearby. Dutch was aware that the brothers did not entertain night time fishing and felt sure that his pursuers would do their homework, making them aware that their best option was a night time approach when no other persons should be present.

He then sorted through the contents of his rucksack and removed the small pre-set vhf frequency radio, together with the four ground motion sensors. Leaving the rucksack, he then descended the hill, and furtively navigated the side of the lake furthest away from the cottage; which was thickly populated by the waterside bulrushes and rhododendron bushes. On reaching the one and only entrance to the property from the road, he placed a motion detector in the earth under the hedgerows on each side of the entrance. Then he tested that they were working correctly by monitoring the radio frequency by his own movement and from the passing cars on the adjacent road. Dutch repeated the same procedure halfway along the drive with the two remaining detectors, but as he wished, due to their range capabilities he discovered that these did not detect any road movement from the passing traffic. He concealed all four in such locations that they would be unlikely to come to notice for a very long time.

On cautiously returning to his equipment, he nominated a secluded location with a good view of the entire property from the edge of woodland. Dutch was aware that his intended hide was situated on Forestry Commission land, which apart from the road, surrounded the Ferguson property. With the pickaxe and spade he began to dig a shallow trench, which without the pickaxe would have proved difficult due to the extensive shallow roots within the dry packed soil. While carrying out the task, he was reminded of how in his past career, during some of the conflicts in which he had been engaged, it had been necessary for him to have prepared similar furrows on occasions for dead bodies. As he dug through the thinner roots of the surrounding oak trees, keeping as quiet as possible and out of sight from anyone below, he was reminded of other past times. While in the army he gained qualification as a sniper, where part of the training consisted of being sent to a precise location, 'digging in' and waiting for a specific target to appear. The wait could be for days, and during the exercise training staff would be observing the target area, in an attempt to locate any movement from the sniper which would reveal his position. To succeed, the sniper would have to be not only observant, but he would also have to be still and awake the entire time and be expected to hit the fleeting target when it appeared. Such thoughts caused him to delve into a side pocket of the rucksack which contained several items from his past military career and to remove a small tube of camouflage cream, which he then proceeded to smear over his entire face.

Once he estimated that his entire frame would fit just below the earth surface, he then placed the sleeping bag inside the trench, spreading the poncho on top. By meticulously arranging all other items from his rucksack around his observation post, he would know exactly where each and every item could be located, even in darkness.

On settling into his clandestine position, Dutch carried out an intense study of the scene below, as in a few hours he would only have the night sight monocular to rely on for any movement. He observed that they were still in possession of the large double-cab pick-up truck parked at the front of the building, but the pristine Ford Mustang parked alongside it appeared to be a new acquisition. He had never been a big fan of flash cars, but since having seen the epic film 'Bullitt' as a youngster, he had admired the way the Mustang handled while being driven at speed by the actor Steve McQueen in a car chase down the steep hills of San Francisco. The only other obvious addition was a modern-looking motor home parked close to the rear of the house in such a manner he was unable to read its registration plates. It initially crossed his mind that it could be occupied by an angler, but then he couldn't imagine that two such unsociable villains would allow a paying customer to park so close to their property with all that he suspected went on there. Especially, when there was a power cable connecting the vehicle to an exterior electricity socket on the wall of the building. As the afternoon proceeded, Dutch observed the brothers moving both outside the cottage and inside of the large glass conservatory, a construction that he had considered in his plotting may assist in him in causing chaos in the near future. Even from his post he was easily able to distinguish between the two brothers, as Popeye was of a stocky build and still supported his shaven head look; whereas Crank was taller, slimmer and with a good head of dark hair.

Dutch's attention was drawn to Crank, when he left the building and knocked on the door of the motor home. As the door swung open; he saw a tall, slim male with short, cropped hair lean out of the doorway and converse with his caller. Following a short conversation, both men went back inside of their respective accommodation, only for both to emerge seconds later, each now carrying what Dutch could clearly see were firearms. Due to the distance away from the pair, he could not identify the exact weapons but could clearly establish that they were both sub-machine guns. Both men became animated as they examined and rehearsed aiming and firing the weapons. While they were engaged in their play-acting, Popeye emerged from the house carrying a shotgun, immediately joining in the jovial conversation. From the shape of the weapon, Dutch thought it to be a single-barrelled pump action shotgun. From the scene that had emerged before him, it seemed that the brothers had quickly taken his warning seriously and had even bought in a 'gun for hire' for a possible confrontation. Dutch was pleased that so far his deception appeared to be working well, especially as he was now conning the conmen, giving them a taste of their own medicine. However, the success of his scheme was now entirely reliant on his suspicion that Nesbitt had passed on the contents of his purported telephone conversation to a taxi company.

After the three gunmen returned to their accommodation and the fishermen had left the grounds, there was little further activity as the evening progressed. Being summer time, it was not necessary for Dutch to use his monocular until late into the evening. As the darkness descended, he would regularly scan the entire scene below him, but he was always confident that during these times the sensors if working correctly would give him the best chance of detecting any uninvited guests. As the night progressed, Dutch was regularly needing to move his cramped body within the trench, finding from time to time the necessity to emerge for a stretching routine. After the lights of both the cottage and the motor home were extinguished, Dutch believed that if he did happen to nod off he could completely rely on the tremble sticks to wake and warn him of any movement on the driveway to the cottage. His thoughts were that at night it would be necessary for any intruders unaware of the terrain and not wishing to use torches to use the driveway, as to enter from any other direction meant the negotiation of hedges and fences; followed by walking noisily through the thick undergrowth in complete darkness.

Just after ten o' clock, with Dutch fully alert, he noticed the light come on in the motor home which immediately caused him to observe the vehicle through his monocular. After only a short period the light was extinguished and the occupant left the vehicle carrying what appeared to be the firearm that he had seen earlier. This person walked around the far side of the house and started to walk towards the road behind a tall hedge that ran adjacent to the gravel driveway. Dutch was unable to fully see the subject due to the height of the hedge, but he was able to trace his progress by the light and shade as he passed behind the minor gaps in the hedgerow in which a ground movement detector was situated. Due to the speed that he moved in the darkness; this person had obviously previously made himself aware of his surroundings. As the shadowy figure approached the detector, Dutch was pleased that the activation was clearly monitored by the radio earpiece hooked over his ear. As the gun-toter approached the end of the drive, he unwittingly gave the detectors another test as the radio signal sounded once more. Although, the passing traffic had been activating the detectors, Dutch now knew that all four were still working perfectly for any pedestrian movement within range of his receiver. The subject of his observation then sat down in the shadows close to the entrance. Dutch continued to observe the figure until he returned to the motorhome via the same route. After briefly entering the vehicle, he emerged still carrying the weapon, and with a bag in the other hand, he made his way to an open-fronted boathouse situated at the side of the lake. Dutch could just about make out from within the shadows that from this position he was sitting intently watching the drive. Throughout the night, approximately every hour the mysterious gunman would walk the same route behind the hedgerow and wait by the entrance before returning to the boathouse. From vapour traces within the boathouse, it appeared the minder was from time to time opening a hot flask. This routine carried on, until dawn, when the unknown man returned to the motorhome, shortly after drawing all curtains.

Dutch had been impressed by the way this person had carried out his duties, thinking that he may later be glad of his presence as he was not sure if the brothers alone would be capable of dealing with members of the organised cartel. The unknown male had been quiet and alert throughout the night, giving the impression that he was a professional, not just someone helping out, doing a one-off favour for his mates. From his conduct and self-discipline, Dutch would not have been at all surprised if this man had once served in the military. The Fergusons must have known him, or he had come with excellent credentials, as they appeared to be solely relying on him for their overnight safety. As was his habit of associating particular song titles to various situations and also to refer to people by a chosen nickname, he mentally dubbed the mystery man as 'The Night-watchman'. From what he had now observed the three men below, like himself and because of his phone call, were all expecting any unwelcomed visitors to arrive during the night. For his elaborate plan to work now solely depended on whether Nesbitt had passed the information to his pursuers. It was a gamble he had to take as he could not think of any other method to settle the matter without direct confrontation, for which he was at the disadvantage as no longer being in possession of a firearm, and he was in no doubt whatsoever that his opponents would be armed.

Dutch, feeling very weary and suffering from eye strain, made himself some food and drink and, following the temporary stowing of his equipment, got into his sleeping bag, turned the radio volume low, pulled the camouflage netting over himself and closed his eyes. His three hours sleep did not prove to be restful, as he had not been required to rough sleep for many years, when his body was much younger and suppler. Although, he was able to clean his teeth, he hated the thought of not being able to wash for several days, at least. As he moved himself out of his cramped and uncomfortable position, he realised that he had been awoken by the two brothers standing by the pickup, in which Crank was sitting in the driver's seat with the engine running. At the conclusion of the conversation, Crank alone drove the truck along the drive and out of his sight, activating all movement monitors as he left. It was Dutch's guess that while they were on alert due to his false information, one of the brothers would remain present on the site at all times until they considered the threat was over.

Dutch suspected that it would be a long uncomfortable day ahead, so in between periods of observation and stretching, he would busy himself around his site and familiarise himself with the map to execute any required quick getaway. As it was now daylight, he was able to tune the radio to BBC Radio Sussex and Surrey, the local radio station that he had regularly listened to before his hasty departure to Venezuela. The combined music and chat helped to relieve the boredom, as for long periods of time there was little activity from below his position.

During mid-morning three anglers arrived at the lake, and although the detectors had signalled the arrival of each of their vehicles, the loose gravel on the drive alone was enough to warn of their approach. On Crank's return, he drove slowly down the drive observing the activities of the fishermen, then once parked he approached the anglers. Following what appeared to be him collecting their fees, with little conversation with either of them, he strode back into the house. His stern unsociable conduct was of no surprise to Dutch as he had previous experience of his inhospitable manner. Dutch, had no interest in fishing, probably because his late grandfather nicknamed Sinbad (due to him once being one of the few Brighton beach-based boat fishermen) always reeked of fish. Because of his occupation, fish was on the menu far too often for young Dutch's liking. Although, he had no enthusiasm for the sport, Dutch took an interest whenever the anglers occasionally reeled in some big fish, being grateful for their presence as there had been little movement from either brother.

During mid-afternoon the curtains of the motor home were drawn open, followed shortly after by the Watchman leaving the vehicle wearing just a singlet, shorts and trainers. He then proceeded to carry out a routine of body stretches, sit-ups and press-ups designed to work out every part of his body. Dutch recognised the series of exercises as those that he had once followed regularly himself but less often in recent years. Following the workout, the Watchman commenced a slow jog along the drive until he reached the road where he turned and ran at a much faster pace back to the building. He carried out these repetitions numerous times, making Dutch envious seeing this man stretching and exercising his limbs while he was wedged into his fox hole. Dutch was pleased that such a fit person had decided that the short drive was the only suitable surface to run on, because if he had decided to run some cross country, he may well have encountered his own observation post.

After completing the running, the Watchman then carried out a warm down routine, making Dutch realise that this man was the 'real deal' and could well be a professional hitman. Having witnessed his physical efforts, it reminded Dutch that he had done little exercise since Melanie had informed him of her suspicions, as he had then spent every bit of his spare time into his planning. He vowed that once he had hopefully rid himself of his pursuers, he would get back into shape.

Dutch saw the Watchman walk into the cottage carrying a towel. The thought of a shower or a bath made him conscious of his grubby existence, causing him to hope that Nesbitt remembered and relayed the full address of the cottage to the interested party and also that he had only hired the cottage for a few days, as he didn't relish the thought of spending too long in the conditions. If they didn't make a move in the next day or so he would have to request Jon to replenish his supplies, and perhaps attempt to get a daytime shower somewhere. Although, he had been constantly vigilant throughout the previous night, he hadn't realistically expected a visit on the first night, for if they were members of an organised criminal gang, they also would require planning and preparation for such a murderous attack.

Once the Watchman had returned to his accommodation and the anglers had left, the late afternoon ticked by slowly for Dutch because of the lack of movement, the only interest being the arrival of a supermarket truck which not only deposited foodstuffs but also a considerable amount of alcohol. Following its departure, he took the opportunity to eat, use the latrine and tidy up his site, keeping everything 'good to go' should he need to make a quick departure. When it became necessary for him to move the catapult and pebbles to a more strategic position, he could not resist taking a number of target shots between the trees behind his location. He was pleased with the relative accuracy that he was able to obtain considering he had not used such a contraption since his childhood. As it became dark, he turned up the volume of the radio, with a view to testing the detectors situated close to the road against any passing traffic. He was now fully prepared for another long vigil during the fine, clear moonlit night.

At a similar time, as on the previous evening, the Watchman emerged from the motor home and began to repeat almost the same routine, concluding with him taking up his sentry post in the boathouse. Apart from the passing traffic and the occasional wildlife triggering the alarms, all remained quiet, leaving Dutch concerned as what to do if once again nothing occurred that night.

His interest was later alerted when he saw the distant headlights of a car travelling very slowly along the public road, almost as if the occupants were searching for something. As this vehicle left his sight behind trees, the movement detectors placed by the entrance activated and sent a continuing signal over his radio, indicating that the vehicle had remained stationary close to the entrance. After a short period, the alarm ceased, indicating that it had moved from the area. Dutch viewed this episode with interest as it appeared that someone was looking for a particular property. From his elevated position and with the aid of his detectors, he had a huge advantage over the Watchman who would have no knowledge of the recent and unusual vehicle movement. The incident caused Dutch to illuminate his watch face, noting the time was 1:20 a.m., less than five minutes had passed when the detectors situated at the entrance were triggered. This caused Dutch's heart rate to race, as there were no obvious car lights to be seen. The detectors then fell silent denoting that whatever or whoever had again moved away. Shortly after, the next set of detectors placed halfway along the drive indicated movement via the radio.

All the radio activity convinced Dutch that this was the moment that he had been waiting so patiently for, which caused him to commence using his monocular to view the furthest section of driveway that was within his sight. It was not long before he could see two dark shadowy figures furtively walking along the drive towards the cottage. As they passed the side of the lake and boathouse, the dark figures continued to move silently on the far side of the drive in the darkness of the shadows of the trees and bushes. As the two moved closer to both the house and Dutch's position, he could now see by the magazine clips that both were carrying what appeared to be AK-7 assault rifles or similar, which indicated to Dutch how well prepared and desperate these men were to eliminate him.

At the same time as the men reached the parked truck and concealed themselves behind its large cab, Dutch noticed a movement in the boathouse. On closer inspection he could see that the Watchman, by his movement, was now well aware of their presence, and on seeing a glimmer of light from his position suspected that he was alerting the brothers by phone of the approaching danger. To confirm his suspicion, just seconds later Dutch noticed a shaft of light appear from under a door from inside the conservatory. The apparent warning from the Watchman pleased Dutch, as he had intended to make a similar call on the 'Burnaphone' which had remained switched off since its one and only call to the address. This phone had now become superfluous to his future-intended actions. The light emitted from the doorway was quickly extinguished, leaving the cottage once again in complete darkness.

Dutch's attention then returned to the Watchman, who had now emerged from the hut and was crossing the drive, creeping slowly down the hedgerow behind the two interlopers. He was confident that such a professional like he thought this man to be would have prepared for such a situation. As both brothers were now anticipating an attack and in possession of firearms, he presumed as soon as any shots were fired both men inside the building would be ready to respond quickly to any incursion. Before the Watchman reached a suitable firing position, one of the intruders hurried from the cover of the truck to occupy a site behind a dilapidated wooden log store at the side of the cottage. This separation left the Watchman in a less advantageous position, and as Dutch only wished one set of winners in the actual battle that was about to commence, he decided to put the cat amongst the pigeons by confusing the raiders and at the same time alerting the brothers. He removed a pair of disposable plastic gloves from his pocket, picked up the readily accessible catapult, and with gloved hands loaded its pouch with one of his chosen pebbles, all of which he had meticulously wiped clean. Then on tightly pulling back the thick elastic, he aimed at the fully glazed conservatory. Once the elastic was fully taut, he let the shot go. He then watched woefully as the propelled pebble missed its target and went unnoticed into the undergrowth.

Disappointed but unperturbed, he immediately loaded and fired the weapon once more, this time smashing a window in the roof of the conservatory, causing a loud shattering sound. Without looking for any reaction from below he repeated the action, on this occasion smashing a side window pane. The sounds of the breaking glass ignited an immediate response, as the exterior lights at the front of the building came on. The bright lights clearly illuminated both the Mustang and the pickup, behind which the other intruder was concealed, causing him to remain motionless and a perfect target for the hidden Watchman.

Almost immediately the lights came on at the front. Dutch saw Popeye exit the rear door of the building situated close to the now damaged conservatory, all of which still remained in darkness. Popeye, holding the shotgun, was trying to conceal his sizeable frame behind a brick-built porch support. Dutch considered that once he moved from the pillar, not being aware of the gunman hidden behind the wood shed, he would become a sitting duck, so once again he loaded the sling and fired at the wood store. The pebble hit the corrugated metal roof of the rotten wooden structure with such ferocity that it penetrated one of the thin rusty panels, causing the hider to break cover and turn to see from where the missile had been projected. The noise caused by the propelled pebble and the grainy sight of a man with a gun caused Popeye to step out from his cover and start blasting away in the direction of the shed. After only one or two of the shots fired by Popeye, Dutch heard the agonising screams of the intruder, which were accentuated by the stillness of the night. Popeye had obviously 'lost it', as even after the fallen man was still and silent, he continued to walk towards him repeatedly firing at what was obviously a dead or incapacitated body. Dutch's first thought was 'what a nutter', bang goes any chance of him making the excuse in law of using only sufficient force to protect himself.

While the shots were being fired, the second trespasser was attempting to peer through the side window of the cab in the direction of the salvo. Following his dispensing of the catapult, Dutch was now, with the aid of the exterior lighting, able to clearly view the parked vehicles unaided by his monocular. He heard the Watchman call out loudly from his darkened position behind the intruder. As far as Dutch could deduce, he had instructed him to drop his weapon, but his warning was ignored and the man turned around and fired haphazardly into the darkness in the direction from where he believed the voice had come. As he did so he made his way round to the other side of the pickup to seek cover, not noticing that he now had his back to Crank who had emerged from the front door, and who seeing his unprotected prey, began firing from the automatic weapon. As the first salvo of bullets hit the victim, he gave out a chilling scream, and like his brother Crank showed no mercy as he fired more than enough rounds into the collapsed and face down lifeless body. Crank then walked towards his victim, picked up the gun that had been dropped by the fallen man, then turned the limp body by lifting it with his boot under the chest and calmly examined the dead man's face.

Crank was soon joined by both Popeye and the Watchman. After a short discussion, the Watchman shook both brothers' hands and walked calmly back to the motor home, having briefly looked in the direction of the body laid near the wood shed as he passed nearby. Considering what had happened only a short time before, his manner was so calm and collected that Dutch felt sure that he was no stranger to such incidents. He had also been very astute, as to how he had the situation covered but saw the opportunity to let the brothers carry out the killings, yet no doubt had been handsomely paid for what was just his mere presence. After entering the living part of the vehicle with his weapon, he emerged shortly afterwards with a set of folding steps. After opening and climbing the steps at the side of the camper, he opened the awning container that ran along the side of the vehicle and placed a wrapped item inside. Dutch knew nothing about awnings but he was certain that to accommodate what had been placed in the container it could not have held what it had been designed for. He was certain that by the shape of what was placed inside that it was the gun. Dutch considered that it was an ingenious place to conceal the weapon and further proved to him that this man was the ultimate hitman. The Watchman then closed and locked the container, and after returning the steps to the living quarters unplugged the power socket. He then calmly entered the driver's cab and drove slowly without lights towards the road, passing the brothers who were hurriedly moving the body that was once laying near the vehicles into the open rear section of the pickup.

Dutch would have liked to watch how the brothers were going to go about their clear-up operation, but it was essential that he was never seen anywhere near the premises. Whatever they planned on doing would have to be quick, as Dutch could see that all the upstairs lights at the front of the semi-detached houses situated almost opposite the entrance of the drive had come on since the commencement of the shootings. He felt sure that even in an area where night time poaching was not uncommon, residents having heard so much rapid gunfire would be alarmed and call for police assistance. Dutch considered that with the mention of firearms the police would scramble armed officers to initially attend the scene, and due to the time of night and the rural location, he estimated that he would have ample time to pack and completely clear his camp of any tell-tale signs of his thirty-six hours occupation of the area. Firstly, he filled in the shallow trench, covering it with twigs and leaves, then did the same to his temporary toilet. Turning on his pocket torch he briefly inspected the areas he had inhabited and satisfied himself that he had returned the ground to its natural appearance. It was necessary not to leave anything at the site, including unused pebbles, which he threw deep into the woods. Once he had placed his fully packed rucksack over his shoulders, with the folded map in one hand; he hurried away from the area following his well-rehearsed exit which he had carefully planned via the public footpaths indicated on the borrowed map.

Chapter 8
Break My Stride (1983)

Artist: Matthew Wilder
Writers: Matthew Wilder, Greg Prostopino

Dutch was confident that even in the darkness he could reach his first destination, the village of Clayton, some four miles away, by following the paths using the silhouettes of the hedges and the tree lines that separated each of the woods and fields. Although, for safety he found it necessary to walk through the short dark wooded areas with their underfoot hazards but on reaching open ground, needing to quickly separate himself from the scene, he broke into a fast pace march through the pastureland, in a method known by paratroopers as 'tabbing', an acronym of 'Tactical Advance to Battle'.

He was about half a mile into his trek when he crashed into a waist-high wire-strand fence surrounding an open field. Presuming the fence had been erected to prevent livestock straying onto other land, he climbed the obstruction, continuing to confidently jog across the open field into the darkness, and heading towards a distant set of tall trees which indicated his intended route. As he strode across the totally black surface, he suddenly felt himself falling through the air, throwing him into total confusion as to what was happening. In the seconds that he remained suspended, he was reminded of the moments of free falling just prior to a parachute opening, during his many previous parachute jumps that he had experienced. As he remained in complete darkness, he had no idea as to what surface he was about to land on, so he attempted to place himself in the best possible position for the inevitable impact. The heels of his boots hit the ground first, and as they immediately slid away on the downward-sloping mud surface, Dutch crashed onto his back, the force of which was predominantly taken by his heavily laden rucksack. As it hit the surface, the force of the impact on his back caused all of the oxygen contained in his lungs to be instantly expelled.

During his previous boxing experiences, both as a student and when competing in armed services competitions, he had been winded many times before but nothing remotely like this. As he lay there motionless, loudly gasping for air to refill his oxygen-starved lungs, his mind was trying to comprehend what had occurred. It took several minutes before he could resume normal breathing. Once he no longer had to concentrate on that, he began to wonder what damage such a heavy fall had done to the rest of his body. His first concern was his entire back, which was causing him intense pain. Knowing that to suddenly move a seriously damaged neck or spine may result in permanent paralysis, he waited for a few minutes to allow the pain and shock to subside before attempting any movement. His first effort while remaining still was to move his fingers in both hands, followed by moving his toes. He felt immense relief as he slowly discovered that despite the pain, he had movement in all limbs and no bones appeared to have been broken.

As the initial pain and shock reduced, he managed to free the rucksack from his back and sit up straight. Having done so, he tentatively searched his jacket pockets for both the mobile phones and the torch, concerned that they all may have been broken due to the heavy impact. Discovering all three intact, he used the torch to illuminate his surroundings, the sight of which initially totally confused him. He was laying on a small mud bank beneath a tall cliff face, on either side of him were large chunks of rock, on which if he had fallen would have resulted in far more serious injury that he had incurred, or even death. His thoughts were; although, he believed he had lost all of his nine lives, he had now experienced yet another lucky escape. From the yellow clay of the cliff walls he knew that he was in a brickyard quarry. He was aware from the map that there was a brickyard nearby, but the quarry excavation was shown to be well away from the field that he had fallen from, which was now above him.

Then realisation dawned upon him. Once again he illuminated the scene with the torch and located the map that had been in his grasp, and which had fallen close by. For the first time since the impact, he moved his entire body to retrieve it. On unfolding the concertina pages he examined the glossy front cover, searching for the date that it had been issued, finding it to be some twenty years old. In view of the time that had elapsed, he came to the realisation that the routes of the public footpaths had been diverted due to the digging of the quarry walls by the clay excavators, which had removed parts of the field that once supported the footpath. Dutch felt a sense of exasperation that when studying the map borrowed from his father-in-law's study, he had not taken such a development into account. He was now aware that the fence that he had climbed had been erected around the field to prevent such accidents, but in the darkness, he had been unable to distinguish between the surface of the field and the blackness of the void below.

Until this point, his scheme had worked perfectly, but now he was lying in a pile of mud, in pain from head to toe, only half a mile from a double killing that he had orchestrated. Desperate to move on, he slowly and painfully got to his feet, looked up to where the skyline met the cliff edge, estimating that the sheer drop was almost forty feet, yet apart from extensive bruising he was relatively unscathed. On surveying the steep dark clay and stone walls that surrounded him, he realised that he would have to find another route to re-join the footpath that he had been following. He could barely see any paths about him but could feel underfoot, the indentations in the mud left by the tyres of what he believed would have been a huge earth excavator. His only exit from the man-made valley was to slowly and painfully follow its tracks between the deep water-filled pits on either side. It was essential that he rid himself of the 'Burnaphone' as soon as possible, as it would show an association with the Fergusons' telephone. With this realisation he took the phone from his pocket, opened it up, took out the sim card, and then encased both separately in balls of damp mud which would help to project both as far as possible. He then, with all his effort, threw both the card and the phone separately into the large watery expanses.

Although, feeling relief at jettisoning the phone, the weight of the rucksack was heavy and uncomfortable on his sore back. However, with each step he consoled himself that a combination of him sliding on the wet mud and his packing of all the rigid items in the side pockets, the sleeping bag, ground sheet and softer items had taken the main impact of the fall, preventing serious injury to his spine. As he made his way towards two very large white open-fronted industrial sheds, illuminated by bright lights both inside and outside of the buildings, he could see that these contained thousands of newly constructed bricks in clamps, stacked expertly for drying over the regulated heat from beneath. Situated in close proximity to the sheds was what appeared to be a brick-built office, in which he could see a lone man sitting at a table, reading a newspaper. In his need to relocate the public footpath, he moved away from the inhabited building, using the abundant lighting emitted from the sheds to once again consult the outdated map. Satisfied that a nearby farm track would lead him to his desired location, he once again continued through the darkness, eventually locating the path just prior to a further farm track that led through a tunnel under the A23 London to Brighton dual carriageway.

After negotiating the tunnel, he turned right onto a farm access road, eventually joining another footpath which led him south of the village of Hurstpierpoint. Early in his planning he had considered walking the short distance to the neighbouring town of Hassocks where there was a railway station on the London to Brighton line. He now considered that because of the success of his plan, as the station was only a few miles from the scene, the police may examine all CCTV situated in a wide circumference and his appearance would stand out significantly amongst the early morning commuters. As he crossed a minor road and continued his journey southwards, although, feeling sore in numerous places; he was now moving more freely and making better progress, despite the occasional tripping over roots and ruts hidden by the darkness. If seen on these remote paths and farm tracks, he would stand out like a sore thumb and anyone sighting him would be suspicious and remember the occasion, but he was now only a mile away from a much wider used pedestrian route.

At one stage, Dutch thought he heard the sound of a distant helicopter, and to remain out of sight he did briefly consider climbing down the nearby embankment and walking through the mile and a quarter long Clayton Tunnel, which would take him in the direction of Brighton, but he realised this would be a dangerous journey with the speeding trains only inches away from him. He considered that in the interval between trains he could move along the tunnel by sheltering in the regular safety recesses constructed in the walls for railway engineers. The sound that he had heard proved to be an approaching goods train, but he had already decided against this option as if he was seen entering or leaving the tunnel, the British Transport Police stationed at Brighton could be on the scene within a short time.

As he emerged from the footpath at the side of the 'Jack and Jill' pub, he looked southwards towards the high horizon. Before him were the two welcome silhouettes of the Jack and Jill windmills, sitting close together on the heights of the extensive area of the South Downs National Park. Although, still four miles from his final destination, he now felt he was finally on home turf, as he had always felt an affiliation with these particular hills ever since Melanie and he had walked their entire length of one hundred miles. On consulting his watch, he noted that it was nearly 4:00 a.m. and due to the clear summer morning sky, the early dawn light assisted him in negotiating the paths leading to the summit. On slumping down at the base of Jack, he drank the last of his water and took the opportunity to dispose of both empty plastic water containers, together with other litter that he had collected from his hide into a convenient nearby waste bin.

Dutch considered that if the police suspected there could be further persons outstanding from the shootings and launched a helicopter, he was still relatively close to the scene. Therefore, he would be vulnerable to such a search by the use of a heat-seeking device, as the next half of his journey would be on open countryside with little chance of concealing himself. Having dismissed the idea of leaving the area by the railway tunnel, he had one final option left open to him. For the sheer effort and inconvenience involved, it was a choice he had not wished to take, but he now felt it necessary to do so.

Only a short walk from the windmills was a place where he could remain completely out of sight both from the land or the air. He had first discovered the location when only about ten years old; both he and his brother Roy had absconded from their school without permission from either teachers or their grandparents. Their truancy was caused by the continual daily humiliation and bullying that each of them, together with their other siblings, received due to their poor and meagre lifestyle under the care of their overwhelmed but loving grandparents.

He approached the innocuous clump of trees situated near the summit on a steep section of the rolling hills, which to any passers-by using the nearby path looked to be a section of uninteresting natural landscape. The copse appeared to be impenetrable woodland entirely surrounded by thick brambles reinforced by barbed wire fencing. It had been over thirty years since he and his brother had last visited the spot, but since then Dutch had taken Melanie there after she had shown an interest during their epic South Downs trek. Although, it appeared that nobody had entered the circle of woodland for a considerable time, he could still remember the best point of entry to reach his intended safe haven. The height of his location, together with the clear night time sky, aided his efforts of hacking through the brambles with a fallen stick. Throwing his haversack over the top of the wire fence, and with the help of the fading battery of his torch, he managed to weave his body in between two of the strands of barbed wire without his clothing becoming snagged. Once through the obstacle. he then pushed his way through further thicket consisting of brambles and stinging nettles.

On reaching the centre of the copse, Dutch saw the large square concrete structure raised above the scrubland. As he stepped up onto the concrete, he could see and feel that the metal entry/exit hatch positioned in its centre was unlocked and partially open. Nearby two controlled air vent pipes protruded from the ground. By standing above the hatch and gripping its robust metal handle, he worked the hatch up and down numerous times in an effort to loosen its movement on its rusty hinges. He always thought that it was strange that the authorities in charge of this land had not found a way of permanently locking the hatch, but at this moment in time he was grateful that he had full access. Once he was satisfied that there was enough movement with the portal, with determined effort he opened it fully, again using his torch light to examine the void beneath. The struggle brought back fond memories of all those years ago when he and Roy as two scrawny kids spent an age together attempting to lift the lid far enough for them to be able to squeeze inside. By kneeling, he was able to confirm that the metal descending ladder was still intact by giving it a robust shake, which showed that it was still safely connected to the wall and the concrete floor some fourteen feet below.

As he began his descent Dutch grabbed his rucksack, using his free hand to hold the ladder as he made his way to the bottom. As he stepped onto the floor, he was pleased that the surface was fairly dry, as he did not relish waiting for hours in a damp environment. Again with his torch he briefly examined the two small subterranean rooms and toilet. The larger of the two rooms was mainly as he remembered it. A single raised metal bedstead remained in a corner, other furniture included a bench, shelves and two folding chairs. The only additions that Dutch noted were some additional litter on the floors and graffiti on the walls, proving that others had also discovered the shelter. He then placed his sleeping bag across the bedframe, gratefully laying himself down upon the hard metal sprung surface which proved uncomfortable in contact with his bruised back. As disagreeable as the situation was, he could now rest and remain out of sight until the time was right to emerge. During the wait he took the opportunity to use the toilet wipes to remove the camouflage paint from his face.

As he lay in half sleep-mode, he thought about his past research as to the reasons why such unusual secret structures had been built. During the mid-1950s, a nuclear threat known as the 'Cold War' caused numerous monitoring posts to be erected in various strategic locations over the UK. Such positions were the responsibility of The Royal Observer Corps and manned by two or three volunteers to monitor any radioactive fall-out caused by a nuclear attack. Many of these bunkers were made redundant during the 1980s following the break-up of the Communist bloc. Most had been filled in or put to another use, unlike this particular excavation which remained largely in its original condition. Dutch considered that such a place would be ideal for a homeless person should it be closer to civilisation, equipped with electricity and have a more sterile supply of water rather than the sheep trough close by.

Dutch did manage to grab some short sessions of sleep and on one occasion heard through the partially open hatch the sound of a distant helicopter, causing him to congratulate himself for his decision to 'stay put' until the world awoke and he would be less conspicuous. It was during this period that his thoughts drifted to how Nesbitt had played such a significant but unsuspecting role in the success and hopefully the finalisation of his dilemma.

The constant noise of the traffic now being emitted from both nearby major roads, together with the early morning light penetrating the stairwell of the bunker through the partially open hatch, acted as a signal for Dutch to prepare for his departure from the subterranean structure.

Feeling hungry and in need of a hot drink, he once again consulted the map and estimated that he was less than an hour's walk from a well-established early opening mobile transport cafe situated in a lay-by on the A27 Lewes road which acted as the natural northern border to suburban Brighton. The thoughts of hot food and beverage, and only being a few hours away from the opportunity to rest his bruised body and get a decent sleep, encouraged him to rise up and continue walking. Leaving the area of the bunker unnoticed, he could now move around the chalk paths with confidence as he encountered other early morning hikers and dog walkers.

As the morning light intensified, and the rising sun began to shine on the many fields scattered below his elevated position, the peace and tranquillity of the scene allowed him to temporarily forget his predicament. His thoughts turned to Melanie and the lyrics of 'Fields of Gold' by Sting, as he and Melanie had early in their relationship, and as a married couple during their trekking the Downs, made love laying in such fields of barley.

Feeling less conspicuous, he was now able to slow his walking pace as he made his way towards the A27 by way of descending the rolling hills that joined the flat footpaths below. On reaching the café, he saw that the lone male staff member was just opening the large refreshment facility. Following a brief amicable conversation, Dutch requested a mug of tea together with both bacon and sausage rolls.

During the short conversation, Dutch was pleased when the cook had presumed that he was a hiker making his way across the Downs, which was exactly the way that he wished to be perceived, as he was well aware that only a few miles north of his location there would still be considerable police activity.

While awaiting his order, he made himself comfortable at one of the nearby white plastic tables. As he was engaged in reading the day-old newspaper which had been laying on the table, Dutch didn't initially pay particular attention to the silver BMW that pulled up in the lay-by close to where he was seated, and he continued reading, doing no more than glancing at the smart vehicle as he had little interest in prestige cars. For him, cars were just a method of getting from A to B. His favourite mode of transport was a van, due to its practical, multi-purpose use.

Moments later, he heard the almost simultaneous sound of two car doors slamming, which caused him to glance up once again. The sight before him caused a bolt-like feeling pass through his entire body as he saw two burly uniformed policemen walking briskly towards him. His mind went into overdrive. How on earth could they have known who he was, or what he had done; had he been seen? What did he do now, run or bluff it out by purporting to be his standby identity of Ben Furminger? If he ran, he considered that he would have to forsake his cumbersome rucksack, as not only would it slow him down but would also make him easy to identify during any police search. On the other hand, if he did discard the carrier and it was forensically examined, if arrested at a later date it may prove that he had been in the proximity of Albourne only a few hours after the shootings.

Just prior to reaching the table at which Dutch was seated, the officers parted, one taking a seat at the table next to him, while the other approached the serving counter and like himself requested teas and breakfast rolls. Dutch, despite now being aware that they were not there specifically to confront him, still remained tense but feigned any interest in them by continuing to read the newspaper. He would glance up from the pages from time to time, noting that the seated cop was briefly scanning the assembled clientele, including himself. Dutch then considered leaving, but as he had only consumed one roll and drunk half of his tea, such a movement may provoke the suspicion of the officers. When the second officer reached his seat with their breakfast meals, their demeanour was such that it was obvious that at the time they were not engaged in any specific assignment and their presence was purely for the purpose of refreshments. At one point, Dutch noticed that one of the cops was visually examining him and taking a particular interest in his rucksack, which was positioned on the seat next to him.

The tranquil early morning quiet was suddenly interrupted by a loud voice of a radio transmission. Dutch was unable to interpret all that was said, only the call sign of Charlie Delta One Zero, but whatever the officers had been alerted to caused them to immediately acknowledge the operator, quickly gulp down their drinks and continue to consume the remainder of their food as they hurried to the parked police vehicle. To Dutch's relief the BMW then sped off into the feeder lane and, with the aid of the siren and the once concealed blue light, filtered into a line of traffic.

With a feeling of relief, and after a satisfying breakfast, Dutch commenced the final leg of his hike. Having a good knowledge of the city and its outlying areas, he made his way through the various estates avoiding the main roads, eventually reaching the home of his sister in Chapel Street. Jeanette was happy to see him again and honoured her agreement that he was able to temporarily stay in her spare bedroom. Knowing something of his previous exploits, she avoided asking him what he had been doing since she had last seen him or why he appeared to have been sleeping outside. Before taking a bath and seeking some welcome sleep, Dutch cleaned and washed the contents of his rucksack. Once satisfied that none of the items could connect or incriminate him in any way to, or near the scene, he asked Jeanette to wash and dry his only set of clothing as soon as was possible. After their reminiscing of the time before their family had been split up, followed by a discussion regarding the planning of overdue visits to their brother and sister, Dutch entered the spare bedroom. After a long relaxing bath, and from a clean soft bed, he dialled Melanie's mobile phone.

His call was answered almost immediately by the familiar excited voice, "Dennis. Where are you? Are you alright?"

"I'm fine. I got back okay and am staying with Jeanette for a while. How's it going…?"

His words were interrupted as her raised voice said, "Oh my goodness you did it, and you're back. How did you do it? Did you have any problems?"

"It went well but I can't discuss it over the phone. How did it go with you all?"

"It's been good, except that I have been sick with worrying if you got back or not. What have you been up to?"

"Getting back here went well. I think I have sorted our problem out, but we will need to move away from this area to prevent any possible recurrences."

"Should I be worried as to how you have, as you say, sorted it out?"

"No. I can honestly say; I wasn't directly involved in stopping the threat."

"I so hope it's all over now. As far as the moving goes, we are all up for it here. We have been looking at properties in the areas we know, and Mum and Dad fancy one with an annexe attached. They are quite willing to sell the bungalow and go in with us to buy one. As you can imagine Jodie loves the countryside here, especially swimming in the lakes."

"That's great news. When do you plan on coming back?"

"If you're sure that we will all be safe now, we just have a few more properties to look at and we can get back. I will bring some photos and the information given to us by the estate agents that we have visited for you to look at. Mind you, all of these preparations depend on what happens if the police ever trace you."

"True. I have come to a decision about that, which we can discuss as soon as you get back. I'm not going back to the bungalow until your return because what you suspected about that drunk Nesbitt has proved to be correct."

"That will be another reason for Mum and Dad to get away from there."

"It's so nice to hear your voice knowing that you are safe and well, and not so far away now. See you in a few days. Let me know when you are on your way so we can arrange to meet. Give my love to your mum and dad. Tell them I am looking forward to planning our move up there. Love you loads. Bye."

"Bye. Love you too, Dennis."

As he rested his head on the soft comfortable pillow, he came to the realisation that his past military life was now well and truly behind him, since he had found that just two days and nights of living in the open had proved far more uncomfortable than when he was a younger man.

Before drifting off to sleep, a rather more disturbing thought came to mind. Although he had not been one to count the kills that he had been responsible for whilst at war, he became aware that he was possibly now accountable for more deaths then when he was as a serving soldier. Although this was a far from pleasant thought, he felt his actions had been necessary, not only to avenge his wife's ordeal and to save another woman from the same fate, but also latterly to protect both his family and himself. Any feelings of remorse were soon dispelled in the knowledge that each casualty was a vicious criminal and whilst alive remained a danger to society.

He hoped that after two troubled years that they were finally safe, as he now looked forward to a new peaceful future.

Chapter 9
Gangsta's Paradise (1995)

Artist: Coolio
Writers: Ivey, Sanders, Rasheed, Wonder

Proving the pistol was safe, Detective Inspector Jeff Woodall of the Sussex and Surrey Major Crime Unit handed the weapon to the keenly observing instructor. Then, together with other officers, they walked back to their private cars which were parked behind the nearby Indian Restaurant, safely away from the privately-owned chalk pit. The now redundant works located in the hamlet of Offham on the outskirts of Lewes proved an excellent isolated venue for a shooting range leased to the Sussex Police. With his firearms training and tour of duty over for the day, and after bidding farewell to his colleagues, he began his homeward journey to the small market town of Steyning. He had thoroughly enjoyed the full day's training and camaraderie in the natural surroundings on a fine summer's day.

Handling firearms of all descriptions had once been daily practice for the man who was once a former Royal Marine Commando. After leaving the Marines, it had been a predictable progression for him to join the police service, as both his father and younger brother were employed in his home county force of Derbyshire, but as his unit had been stationed in the South of England he applied and was accepted by the Sussex force. His first posting was to Crawley New Town, where he met his future wife, Susan, and had a happy marriage that resulted in their three daughters Lauren, Kirstie and Chloe. Following general patrol duties as a uniformed constable, he transferred to the

CID, the work of which he both enjoyed and excelled at. During very successful spells with this department, he was often directly responsible for leading his team, not only in detecting numerous serious crimes but also reducing the crime rate figures within the division. His enthusiasm and an eye for a thief earned him swift promotion to sergeant, followed by the rank of detective inspector attached to the combined forces major crime investigation department.

On arriving home, while Susan was preparing their evening meal, he took the opportunity to cut the lawns of their modern semi-detached property. Even though all of their daughters had married and moved out several years before, the couple still missed their presence and the sense of family unity when all were seated around the dinner table, each discussing their respective daily events. Jeff would always enjoy his daughters' high hopes and youthful optimism, but his military experiences and now his police work had caused him to become somewhat pessimistic about life in general. However, he was forever mindful not to always give his honest opinion and spoil their dreams and aspirations. Following their meal, then watching a movie, the couple fell sound asleep shortly after going to bed around 10:30 p.m.

The ring tone of the song 'Insomnia' mockingly sounded loudly on the bedside table. The inspector's hand reached out from the bed into the darkness of the still room, grabbing the noise emitter and fumbling to press the receiver button, which when activated illuminated the screen showing the time as 1:59 a.m. He wearily placed the phone to his ear saying somewhat abruptly, "Yeah. Jeff Woodall." As he spoke in his semi-conscious state, he was certain that it would be a call-out. He cursed his luck, as it was his final night on the call-out roster, and up until that moment his designated nights had remained undisturbed.

The familiar voice of the caller said, "Sorry to disturb you, guv. It's Dave Whitcomb at Force Ops Room. I understand that you are the call-out supervision officer for your department tonight."

"Hi, Dave, long time no see. Unfortunately, you are correct, it is me on call. What's the problem?"

"I may be jumping the gun by calling you now, but shots have been fired out at Albourne, and due to the possible individuals involved there is a concern that this could potentially be a serious incident. We don't know the full facts yet, as we are waiting for an armed unit to assemble before any approach is made to the property in question. I thought I would give you an early warning in case it all kicks off."

"So, nobody at present has been seen with a weapon? Just shots heard. Could it possibly just be poachers?"

"From what we have so far it looks like more than that. At 1:42 a.m. the force incident room received several treble nine calls from residents living in the proximity of Lakeside Cottage, Birchwood Road, Albourne, reporting the sounds of numerous gun shots. Due to the nature of the reports it was decided to contain the surrounding area by mobile patrols, until an armed unit was able to attend the precise location. Luckily enough, a traffic car was only a short distance away at Handcross when they received the call, so they were in the vicinity within minutes. After identifying the property concerned, which by the way is also a fishery, they took up a watching brief from a nearby field entrance. Shortly after their arrival they saw the headlights of a vehicle driving from the cottage towards the public road. When this vehicle, which the officers identified as a dark coloured pick-up, reached the road, they suspect that the driver saw the marked police vehicle, as it then reversed at speed, turned around and drove back in the direction from which that it had come. Neither vehicle nor the occupants have been seen since. I have carried out a voters' register check on the address which shows a Michael and Daniel Ferguson living there. There is no trace of those names with local intelligence but checking the names on PNC (Police National Computer) they could be identical to brothers Michael Derek Ferguson and Daniel James Ferguson who both have a string of serious convictions going back years."

"What have they got form for?"

"That's what makes this incident more concerning, because between them they have numerous previous stretching back years, including robbery, G.B.H. and interestingly, firearms offences. Apparently they head a notorious London East End gang but can't confirm it's definitely them until we obtain their dates of birth."

"If it does turn out to be them, any idea why we haven't got any local intelligence on them?"

"If them, their previous address is in Essex, but the majority of their offences were committed in the Met. Perhaps, they have moved into the sticks to avoid some heat and just haven't come to our notice yet. Their life of crime must have paid well as, despite all of their many convictions, as knowing the area like I do, that property must have cost an arm and a leg. The worry is they may have started a gang war on our manor."

"Christ I hope not, Dave, we've got enough to get on with at the moment. There's no doubt that an armed unit is required to effect entry here. Have we an eta for them yet?"

"Not yet, sir. The incident is very recent. I have also called both of the informants who live in the two of the tied cottages situated almost opposite the entrance to the Ferguson residence. One being the gamekeeper for the large country estate, who having previous military service tells me he is very experienced in handling many types of firearms. He categorically states that the first shots that he heard were discharged from a semi-automatic shotgun, or more than one shotgun, as there were at least five continual discharges without reloading. His first thoughts were that there were poachers about, until he heard what he thought was a human scream. Almost, immediately after this he heard a salvo of shots followed by what this time he was absolutely certain were further agonising shrieks, also from the same area. As it was a warm night with his bedroom windows open, he could definitely identify these shots as being fired from an automatic weapon. He is adamant about that. Soon after this he is sure that he heard a vehicle leave the drive opposite, but when he looked out of the window, he couldn't see anything in either direction and believes that it was driven away without any lights on. Later, following his call to the police, he also saw the pick-up drive up the Ferguson driveway to the road, then immediately reverse and drive back, confirming what the traffic guys saw. I have also spoken to his next-door neighbour, who was able to say that shortly before the sounds of the shooting he was awoken by a car being parked in an entrance to a track leading into nearby woods. He originally took no notice of this, as it is a regular parking place for courting couples, and remained in bed, but because of the shots he then checked out of his window and the car is still there, but he is not sure if anyone is inside it or not. I've told him to stay away and leave it to us."

"You say there was a vehicle believed to have left the premises without lights soon after the shots were heard. Any more info on that? It's of vital importance as there is no doubt that whoever that was did not want to be seen or hang around for our arrival and must at least know what has happened there."

"Unfortunately, guv, neither witness could say if it turned left or right out of the drive, because of it having no lights on, but they did think it sounded as being bigger than the average car. Having had radio contact with the traffic unit, they state that once leaving the A23 and joining Birchwood Road, they saw no vehicles whatsoever travelling in either direction. The first that they saw was the pickup. I have also informed all Sussex and Surrey patrols of the incident and requested stop searches on any likely vehicles."

"Thanks for that, Dave. It certainly sounds as if something serious has gone down there, what with vehicles driving off without lights, and someone not wanting to be confronted by the traffic unit. If it does turn out to be them, from what you say they couldn't lawfully hold any firearm as they would probably be disqualified by way of previous convictions. It does seem that it could potentially be a job for us, even if it turns out to be a low-level incident, if it is those two who are now living on our patch, there will be an opportunity to gain some vital intelligence. Tell whoever is in charge of the Specialist Operations Group to liaise with me at Burgess Hill Police Station. It's quiet there and not too far from the target address."

"Will do, guv."

Following the call, the inspector quickly showered, dressed, at the same time apologising to his wife, who he could see from the illumination of the bedside lamp was stirring from sleep. Sue, having been married to the policeman for twenty-one years, was well versed in her husband's nocturnal activities, but pleased that such disruptions since his deployment to a plain clothes specialist department were far less than when he was working irregular hours as a uniformed officer.

In less than twenty-five minutes, Woodall and the SOG team were assembled at the Police Station and logged onto Google maps, studying both aerial and ground images of Lakeside Cottage and its surrounding land. Following a short briefing, with an agreed procedure, the specialist group together with the DI left the building for the short drive to Albourne. After quietly parking their vehicles at the sides of the road, the police contingent, headed by armed officers, made their way as silently as possible towards the black Ford Mondeo which was parked off the road in the entrance to a narrow woodland path only a short distance from the entrance to Lakeside Cottage. The car was found to be fully secure and unattended. The officers manning the nearby traffic patrol car were, together with an armed officer, assigned to wait with the vehicle in case the former occupants should return to it. The registration number was passed to the force control room for enquiries into the ownership of the vehicle. Within a matter of seconds, the Police National Computer revealed that it was registered to a car and van rental company at an address in Battersea in London. The remainder of the group then moved as quietly as possible through the entrance and down the gravelled surface driveway towards the Ferguson residence, unknowingly passing Dutch's hidden; now redundant, ground movement detectors.

On their arrival at the cottage, and when certain that armed officers were in position around the building, the officer in charge of the unit called over his loud hailer, firstly, identifying himself and then requesting any occupants to come out the front door individually with their hands in the air. Only moments had passed when, as instructed, the formidable frame of Popeye emerged from the door barefoot, wearing only a singlet and track suit bottoms. He was then instructed to walk forwards until he reached officers who immediately ordered him to get down on both knees, they then searched him and placed him in handcuffs. Following further police commands, he was shortly followed by his taller, slimmer brother Crank, who was wearing a claret and blue West Ham football club shirt, knee-length cargo shorts and was also barefoot. After being subjected to the same procedure as his brother, they both stood together, remaining silent until Woodall addressed both of them saying, "We have received reports of shots being fired from these premises about half past one this morning. What do either of you know about this?"

The brothers looked at each other and with a barely detectable nod of his head Popeye replied, "Alright, it will cost me a bit of bird but if it gets you all out of here, it was me. I got up to have a piss as I had a few drinks, last night. Went into the conservatory cos I couldn't sleep and saw that fucking fox that has been shitting all over the place. You know how that stuff stinks, so I got the shotgun and gave him a few blasts. It certainly doesn't warrant you lot turning up armed to the fucking teeth."

Ignoring his comment, and smelling alcohol on his breath, the DI said, "Your name is?"

Popeye replied firmly, "Michael Derek Ferguson, date of birth April 29th, 1968."

"Seems you may have gone through this procedure before, Michael."

"You'll soon find out when you look me up."

"How many shots did you fire?"

"Don't know. As I said I had a few drinks."

"Did you hit the fox?"

"Don't know, couldn't be bothered to look."

"Where was it?"

"Can't remember, it was dark."

"Where is the shotgun now?"

"I thought some nosey bastard might blow the whistle, so just in case I chucked it in the channel of water under the rowing boat in the boat house. You now know all you need to know."

Following a request from Woodall, the officer in charge of the armed unit handed his weapon to a colleague, took some disposable gloves from his breast pocket, and having put them on he and a colleague entered the boathouse. After they moved the small craft, one of the officers discarded his body armour, rolled up his shirt sleeves, and with the aid of torch light laid face down on the wooden plank floor, immersed his arms fully into the dark shallow water, and commenced a fingertip search in the silt below. He extricated two submerged broken planks of wood and then he hauled up a clean intact shotgun. The finder then returned to the gathering, carrying what he had now identified as a Beretta pump action shotgun.

On viewing the weapon, the DI directed his question to Michael Ferguson, "Is this the shotgun that you fired tonight?"

"Yep, that's it."

"Are you both certain that there are no further firearms or ammunition in the house or on these grounds, anywhere?"

Crank, standing only a few feet away from the DI, looked into his eyes and in an intimidating manner with a raised voice said, "My brother has coughed to shooting at a fucking fox. No there's no more guns or ammo here, so now do what you've got to do and fuck off out of here with your bunch of clowns."

Unperturbed by his intimidating manner, Woodall stated, "We have been told by someone who has a good knowledge of guns that there was also an automatic weapon fired from here shortly after the shotgun was heard."

Popeye replied, "That's a load of bollocks. Whoever said that knows fuck all about guns, as I only have that shotgun."

"We have been further told that following the shots, cries of pain were heard coming from here."

"Pain! That was me cursing that fucking fox."

"Where did you get the shotgun from?"

Crank quickly interjected, "He found it in the woods a couple of days ago. A poacher dropped it when we were chasing him."

Woodall, with his knowledge of various types of guns, proved that the damp pump action weapon was safe and void of ammunition, before he closely examined it. After doing so he said, "Because this particular shotgun is also semi-automatic and holds more than three cartridges, it is required to have a certificate issued under section one of the Firearms Act 1968. Have either of you got a valid firearms or shotgun licence?"

Popeye replied, "No. I know I'm in the shit. Nick me and get on with it. This has nothing to do with my brother, I found it, and he's never fired it. Get me to the nick soon as I'm in need of a kip."

"Was this loaded when you apparently found it?"

"Yeah, fully loaded with five cartridges and I let that filthy animal have all of them."

On closer examination of the weapon, Woodall saw that from scour marks on the breech of the gun it appeared that the serial number had been forcibly erased. This discovery caused him to say to Michael Ferguson, "I am aware of where the serial number is usually stamped on most shotguns and there does not appear to be one on this one, but there are marks where I believe the number has been completely removed."

"Well there you go, that slippery poacher was far trickier than we thought."

"You say that you found the shotgun. What steps have you taken in reporting the incident and the finding of it to the police?"

"You're fucking joking mate. Exactly the same thing would have happened as what's occurring now. You would have looked us up, expected the worse and gone through this waste of fucking time."

"What did you intend to do with it then long term?"

"Once I had fulfilled my ambition of killing that shitty stinking fox, I would have cut it up with our angle grinder."

"Have you got any previous convictions for firearms offences?"

"A long time ago. What difference does that make?"

"Then you obviously know the seriousness of offences involving firearms."

"Don't give me a fucking lecture now. Let's all just piss off out of here and I'll plead guilty to the whole lot. Let's go now before I change my mind. Satisfied, now?"

He then turned around and started walking towards a convoy of recently parked police vehicles.

Woodall said, "Hold on. You seem in a rush to get us out of here. I haven't finished yet."

Ferguson stopped and turned saying, "I have. Let's go."

Woodall then said to Michael Ferguson, "I am arresting you on suspicion of theft of a shotgun, being in unlawful possession of a firearm, and being in possession of a firearm whilst under the influence of alcohol. You do not have to say anything, but it may harm your defence if you do not mention when questioned something which you later rely on in court. Anything you do say may be given in evidence."

Ferguson replied, "Whatever. Let's go and bring that bunch of muppets with you."

Michael Ferguson was then escorted to a waiting police vehicle, shouting as he went, "Come on now you lot, you can all piss off back to the pig sty." Once contained in the vehicle he was then conveyed to the nominated custody suite situated in Brighton.

Chapter 10
Forensic Evidence (1994)

Artists: Stiff Little Fingers
Writers: Bruce Foxton, Jake Burns

The DI, feeling content that he had dispatched one of the loud-mouthed duo, then turned his attention to Daniel, "Following the shots being heard, a pick-up truck was seen to travel up your drive towards the road. On reaching the road it was then reversed, turned around and driven back down. Why was this?"

"As Mick had woken me up by firing that gun and he was pissed, we decided to go to an all-night petrol station and get some grub. I was driving but when I saw the cop car, I knew they would give us a tug so I turned around, as I thought that it wasn't worth the aggro."

"Are you aware of any further firearms or ammunition being either in the building or on your grounds?"

"No. What do think this is, a fucking armoury?"

"Your brother has been arrested for offences which empowers us under section 18 of The Police and Criminal Evidence Act 1984 to search these premises. I plan to do this straight away. At this stage you are not under arrest. Do you understand?"

Ferguson, whose face then became reddened and contorted, causing the sinews in his neck to become prominent, pushed his face forwards, almost nose to nose with the DI, and shouted loudly, "Why do you coppers always have to push your luck? You've got your nick, you've got the gun, what the fuck else do you expect to find here?"

Again Woodall didn't flinch from his intimidating stance and firmly replied, "I suggest you calm yourself down. The reason for this search is that I suspect that there has more gone on here tonight than we are aware of at present. If not then you have nothing to worry about. If you obstruct our search you will be arrested."

Ferguson taking a step back replied, "That's a fucking laugh that is. We've had all this before. You won't find anything so you'll plant something. You're all the fucking same."

"Right," said the DI addressing all officers gathered in the lit area at the front of the house. "If two of you could accompany Mr Ferguson throughout the search while the remainder have a preliminary look around the house and grounds."

The DI then assigned two officers to check the inside of the cottage for any obvious signs of a disturbance, while the uniform patrol sergeant present arranged a torch lit search around the immediate circumference of the building by the recently arrived divisional patrol officers.

The DI then asked Ferguson, "Where is the pickup that was seen driving back here?"

"I'm not saying anymore. You're really pissing me off now."

"Well we know it didn't come back out onto the road, so unless there is another way out it must be here." He then asked the armed unit inspector to arrange a search for the missing pickup truck.

The two officers who had previously entered the cottage returned to the DI. After a short conversation away from the hearing of Ferguson, the DI said to him, "Although, there are no signs of a disturbance in the main rooms of the house, why have two panes of glass been smashed in the conservatory; and the glass and the stones that appear to have been responsible for the damage remain on the floor?"

"I told you I'm not answering anymore of your pointless questions. All this shit over a fox."

An officer then returned to the DI and informed him of finding the damage and the shotgun pellets in the wooden walls of the woodshed. The DI accompanied the policeman to a corner of the structure and under torch light could clearly see the recent damage and numerous small lead pellets imbedded in the rotting wood. He also noticed that the ground in the immediate area was wet, yet the rest of the surface around it was dry. This caused him to take the officer's torch, and to crouch down, closely examining the grassy surface around the recently watered area. Under the strong artificial light, he could see what appeared to him to be spots of blood on some of the blades of grass. He then instructed the officer to cordon off a wide area around the woodshed with incident tape.

The DI returned to Ferguson, "I believe that I have found shotgun pellets and blood on and around the woodshed. Do you know anything about that?"

"He told you he shot at a fox. I guess as pissed as he was, he still managed to wing it."

"It appears someone has very recently washed the area where the blood is. Who was that?"

"Load of bollocks. It's always wet around that shed."

Before Woodall could respond to his comment, an armed officer returned to the DI requesting that he accompany him to an area situated halfway along the drive. On reaching the armed inspector, the DI was shown a black pickup truck which had been driven deep into thick, tall rhododendron bushes, where some of their broken branches had been placed over the rear of the vehicle to shield it from view. After pushing his way through the tangle of damaged branches towards the rear of the vehicle, a further officer present pointed his torch into the rear open back of the truck. The illuminated area showed a completely empty open metal flat-bed panel. There were no contents on or attached to the sides of the compartment and it was evident by the remaining liquid that the base and sides had recently been doused with water. One of the officers present then drew the DI's attention to both the offside side panel and door of the truck, where he saw a number of large clumps of mud, spread separately across the bodywork. Having gained his attention, the same officer peeled off one of the clods to reveal a small neat hole in the metal body work consistent to that of a bullet hole. The DI noted that the entire circumference of each hole was shiny, giving the appearance of recent damage. The same officer then repeated the process by removing another piece of earth revealing an identical hole. Woodall then instructed that nothing further was to be touched either on or around the vehicle until the arrival of the scene investigators. The DI allocated an officer to stay with the vehicle, and together with the remainder of the party, returned to where Daniel Ferguson was standing with his escort and said to him, "There is a black pickup truck hidden in the bushes just up the lane. Whose is it?"

"Joint ownership. Me and Michael. Why?"

"Because it's half-hidden in the bushes on your land with what appears to be recent bullet holes in one side."

"That's easy to explain. Just after Mick had the row with that fox, some geezer drove down our drive and sprayed the side of the truck with some serious automatic weapon. We only had the shotgun, so had no chance and legged it inside. He must have had some problem with us but never did any more, just drove off."

"So, why hide the truck if you have nothing to hide?"

"Because we knew someone would hear the shots and you lot would pay a visit, see the truck and we would get all this shit. Just like what's happening now."

"You must have some idea who would do something like that?"

"Not really. We have mixed with some naughty boys in the past and probably upset some, but that's all behind us now. We moved here to get away from all that bollocks, but it looks as if it's not as easy as just moving our gaff."

"Why has the rear floor of the pickup been, very recently, thoroughly washed and lumps of mud placed over each bullet hole?"

"Regardless of all that had happened in that short time, Michael, who was pissed, insisted on going to get some food. He was going to drive and I wasn't going to let him, and I certainly wasn't going to drive out with obvious bullet holes in the side. So, we put mud over the holes to hide them. Mick, being pissed, dropped a load of mud on the cargo floor, so I hosed it off before it dried. When I got to the road, I saw the Bill car and didn't want the aggro, so turned around and drove it into the trees hoping you lot wouldn't see it and give us all this fucking bollock."

"Do you really expect me to believe that someone comes down your drive, fires an automatic weapon into the side of your truck, then almost immediately after you drive out with the intention of getting some food?"

"I tend not to argue with my brother when he's pissed and hungry, regardless of the situation."

"Witnesses believe that a vehicle without lights drove out of your drive shortly after the shooting. Who was that?"

Daniel Ferguson excitedly replied, "Yeah, see I told you. That was the car that shot our motor up. I told you that but you don't believe me, now you have the proof."

"I'm sorry but that proves nothing until we find the occupants. For all I know the persons in that car may have been associates of you and your brother."

"That's the response I would expect from the likes of you lot, always trying to take us down any way you can."

"So, you are telling me that your brother started shooting at a fox about 1:30 this morning with an unauthorised shotgun, that he just happened to find a few days ago but didn't bother to hand it in. Then coincidentally, almost at the same time, an unknown person enters your grounds and fires an automatic weapon at your truck and immediately leaves the scene, but unperturbed by that you intended to go and get food until you saw the patrol car."

"Spot on. But as usual you don't believe it, that's why we tried to cover up the holes."

"Well I'm sorry but I don't believe a word that you are telling me. I am going to arrange a thorough widespread search of both your house and grounds to establish exactly what happened here this morning."

"What are you, some kind of fuckwit? We are the victims here. You are going to hear a lot more about this."

After only a short time, a divisional officer searching a weeded area situated behind a large storage container requested the DI's attendance. On joining the officer, Woodall's attention was drawn by torchlight to the charred remains of a fire.

He could see by the beads of water and a wetness around the area that it had been recently extinguished. He picked up a nearby stick and carefully poked a tunnel into the black sticky debris, from which a vapour was released. Woodall then placed his hand over the bore hole that he had created and detected a heat. As he examined the ashes, he could clearly see scorched, melted shoe soles, remnants of a blue denim material and the metal primer caps of shotgun cartridges.

This discovery led him to return to Ferguson saying, "You have seen me looking behind that container where there are remains of a recent fire. It appears that shoes, possibly jeans and shotgun cartridges have very recently been burnt there. Who lit it and why?"

"Me. Just old stuff we didn't need. The cartridges were those Mick fired at the fox."

"I noticed that both of you had bare feet when we arrived, had you and your brother just burnt the shoes that you were wearing at the time of the shooting incidents?"

"Why the fuck would we do that?"

"You know perfectly well why. If something serious has happened here this morning, and someone wished to avoid any forensic connection to the offence, one method would be to destroy clothing and footwear by burning."

"That's just the way you coppers see it. You are trying to make it look like we are trying to hide something. The last time I looked there is no law about what time we can burn our rubbish on our own land."

DI Woodall then made arrangements for a search team adviser, a specialist search dog, (referred to in police jargon as K9), together with crime scene investigators, to be informed to attend the scene as soon as was possible. He made further arrangements for other officers to relieve the armed unit, whose expertise would soon no longer be required.

During their wait, some of the armed officers carried out a cursory search of the interior of the cottage in an effort, for the safety of all present, to locate any further firearms. Soon after beginning the search, one of those deployed approached the DI carrying a small cardboard box. On examination of the brightly red and yellow coloured carton, Woodall saw a picture of a shotgun cartridge. On opening the box, he saw that it contained twenty live cartridges.

Exhibiting the box before him, the DI approached Ferguson, who was sitting in a chair observing an officer engaged in probing the contents of a kitchen cupboard.

The DI asked, "This box containing twenty shotgun cartridges has just been found lying on the floor under some jackets in the hallway cupboard. Who do these belong to?"

"They were there when we moved in here. Didn't know what to do with them, so we left them there."

"Have either you or your brother used any of them?"

"No."

"So, it's a coincidence that the now empty shotgun that your brother supposedly found and fired tonight holds five cartridges and there are five missing from this box that initially contained twenty-five. I'm sure that I could see some remains of cartridges in that fire, so it will be interesting to see if they match with those missing from this box."

"They are a common make, so it would prove fuck all."

"I asked you earlier if you had any further ammunition here and you never mentioned these."

"No, I forgot about them as they weren't ours."

"On your own admission you are not the holder of a shotgun certificate; therefore, you would not be able to

147

obtain these cartridges legally. You were given the opportunity to tell me about them, but you failed to do so. We had to search to find them and I don't believe that such dangerous items would have just been left here. I am, therefore, arresting you on suspicion of theft of the cartridges and being in unlawful possession of ammunition."

After being formally cautioned Ferguson replied, "I've told you the truth. Has anyone told you that you are a complete and utter arsehole?"

Woodall ignored his remark and made arrangements for the prisoner to be handcuffed and escorted to the cells at Burgess Hill Police Station, in order to keep the brothers apart prior to their respective interviews.

After Ferguson's departure from the scene, and as the initial limited search had failed to locate any further firearms or ammunition, Woodall continued to make arrangements for a comprehensive search of the cottage and the entire grounds using specialist units during the daylight hours. Later, on the arrival of relieving officers, the armed unit left the scene, leaving Woodall to inform the incoming teams of the morning's events and the particular sites that he required to be left preserved and undisturbed until the arrival of the scene investigators.

Once satisfied all was in place, Woodall left Lakeside Cottage to attend a hastily arranged briefing with a specialist search team at Brighton Police Station where Michael Ferguson was detained. On his arrival there, after making himself a strong black coffee, he began to draw a map of Lakeside Cottage and its surrounds on the large whiteboard. When all the searchers were assembled, the fully equipped unit remained firmly focused on his recollections of the morning's events. Having been given the facts, Police Sergeant Duffell, the unit's supervising sergeant, referring to Woodall's hand-drawn map, allocated officers to close search particular sections of both the cottage and the grounds.

The DI then approached the allocated exhibit officer, DC Rick Allard, and handed him an exhibit bag containing the

Beretta shotgun, together with another bag containing the box of cartridges. The officer made an entry of each item into the exhibits register, retaining them both for secure storage.

Following the departure of the search team and the K9 handler, Woodall made his way to the custody suite and spoke to the custody sergeant to discuss the detention of Michael Ferguson.

As the prisoner had requested a solicitor, there would be a delay before an interview could take place, so Woodall found a quiet office and began writing his notes regarding the morning's events. While recording his recollections of all that took place and making and receiving numerous telephone calls, he was continually hoping that the search would find something to confirm his suspicions before the interviews with the Fergusons took place. During this time, he was informed that the manager of the car hire company which owned the Mondeo that still remained near the scene had been interviewed by a Metropolitan police officer. He discovered that the vehicle had been hired the previous day for one day only, with a driving licence stolen during a burglary in Surrey the previous year. The staff at the company were not particularly helpful, and were almost indifferent as to the circumstances surrounding the possible abandonment of their vehicle. The company had a reputation for being patrons for the criminal fraternity and were suspected of hiring out cheap cars with the briefest of questions asked. Local police officers had thought for some time that their clientele paid additional undisclosed money as the vehicles hired were often involved in accidents or police pursuits, but despite these incidents the company still appeared to be financially sound. The DI was further informed that the company was currently under investigation by the police and other interested agencies regarding the legality of their practices. The only description given by the company employee of the hirer of the abandoned Mondeo was a male, thirty to forty years of age, medium height, medium build, short black greased-back hair; and of dark swarthy appearance with a strong Eastern European accent.

Woodall had no sooner terminated the call when another call came into the office. On this occasion it was a member of the search team reporting that on the gravel surface close to the parked Mustang, they had located a specific area that was wet and appeared to have been recently brushed over. Due to this anomaly, the team had collected and bagged all brushes for further examination. This discovery had caused the Mustang to be moved and underneath was found a single discharged shell case consistent with a bullet compatible with an automatic rifle. A discussion then took place between the officer and the DI to the effect that this find now confirmed what the gamekeeper had heard. As he had reported a salvo of shots from such a weapon, and with only one shell case found, this gave the impression that the other discharged casings had been located and removed from the area. Possibly due to the haste of a clear-up operation, the shell case under the car had been missed. The location of the one remaining shell case also gave doubt that the automatic weapon had not been discharged from the position further up the drive, as Daniel Ferguson had indicated.

All of this incoming information was excellent news for Woodall, as it confirmed that there was something fundamentally wrong with both brothers' explanations, but he still had no idea as to what exactly had occurred there, only that all of these facts compounded his suspicions that something much more sinister had happened. As the finding of the shell casing further confirmed that an automatic weapon had been fired there, and the strong possibility that it was still on the premises, Woodall's thoughts turned to the nearby expanse of water and the urgent requirement for the attendance of the force diving unit.

At his request, other members of the major enquiry team arrived at the scene. Although, at this stage the offences so far did not reach their criteria, Woodall felt sure some evidence of serious crime would eventually come to notice, and that at the very least the intelligence gained from a thorough investigation into two such prominent villains would prove invaluable.

As he mulled over his next course of action he received a further call from the search team coordinator, and what he was told shocked even the battle-hardened DI 's expectations as to what had occurred there that morning.

He listened intently as he was informed that during the search of the wider grounds, officers had begun lifting three separate manhole covers. On removing the cover to the large sewer inspection chamber, officers were confronted by two male bodies which had been lowered inside. Life was very obviously extinct with both, but a doctor had been summoned to confirm death. Early photographs had been taken of the gory discovery by the scene investigators already in attendance, and it appeared that both had died from being shot, one by numerous bullets and the other by shotgun blasts. Woodall then requested to speak to the senior scene investigator, and once procedures were put in place, he terminated the call and immediately contacted his immediate boss, DCI Tony Byrne.

Byrne, knowing Woodall had been 'flat out' since the early hours, assured him that he would inform all the necessary parties and arrange additional investigating officers to be seconded to the case. Woodall, previously feeling tired, was now pumped full of adrenalin and anticipation. He informed the custody sergeants at the two stations where the brothers were incarcerated of the findings, then together with DC's Gary Bye and Kevin Reay returned to the scene of the now obvious crime.

Shortly after their arrival and in their presence, scene investigators lifted and removed the bodies from the sewer chamber. The recovery operation was filmed for evidential purposes. After their extraction, the pockets of both fully dressed corpses were searched and the only item found on the smaller, stockier dark-haired male was a single ignition key with a key fob bearing the name of the car and van company that owned the Mondeo, which had been parked and abandoned close by.

The accompanying body was that of a taller man, slimmer, with thinning hair, and both appeared to be of a similar age. There was nothing further to identify either and their hands were covered in bags by the forensic team for firearms-connected residue examination, and for the possible requirement of identification by fingerprints.

The finding of the ignition key caused DC's Reay and Bye to approach the nearby Mondeo and, both wearing evidence-preserving gloves, entered and searched the vehicle which appeared to contain no personal property until they lifted the front mats on both sides of the car. Under the nearside passenger floor mat, there was a large bunch of keys, some coins and a wallet containing a large amount of cash, bank and business cards in the name of Yannis Stanescu, giving an address of a South London car valeting company and mobile telephone number. Under the driver's mat there were also some coins, keys and a wallet containing a smaller amount of money with personal papers and cards in the name of Alexe Gheata. This information was relayed to Woodall and arrangements were made to have the car transported by a recovery vehicle to a pound for further forensic examination.

Woodall, realising that according to the names discovered in the Mondeo, the two deceased were most probably of Eastern European origin, which could throw up many delays and complications. He would require an efficient experienced hand to expedite the required procedures, so he made a call.

The call was answered, "Good afternoon, Licensing Officer Sergeant Ahmed Ramiz speaking. How may I help?"

"Hi Ram, Jeff Woodall, here. Long-time no see, how are you doing?"

"Fine thanks, sir. How may I help on this fine day?"

"Ram, I need a good man to help me, but I couldn't find one, so I came to you instead."

"Charmed, I'm sure."

"Only joking, mate. In fact it's entirely the opposite as I require your considerable knowledge and expertise. Are you aware what's happening down here at Albourne?"

"No sir, I've been stuck in my office at Horsham all day."

"Very briefly there was reports in the early hours of numerous shots coming from a cottage belonging to a couple of villains. Following a major search of their grounds, two bodies have been found in a sewer inspection pit. Both men have been recently shot and they could well be Eastern Europeans. As you well know from your vast previous experience as coroner's officer, the identification and repatriation of foreign nationals can cause complications and unnecessary delays in the case moving forward, unless the person dealing with this part of the enquiry fully knows the ropes."

"Am I missing something? Why are you telling me this? I'm now a licensing officer."

"Ram. If I could swing it with your super, could you help us out by being the coroner's officer on this job? I know of your reputation with this sort of enquiry, so it shouldn't take you long to see it through and would take a load off of the team."

"If you can get the authorisation, I would be glad to be of service. I have dealt with several similar overseas-connected deaths and still have numerous connections in many useful departments. It will give me a welcome break from dealing with licensing and gaming activities."

"Thanks Ram, you're a good man. I will speak to Mr Godwin, he's an old mate and I'm sure he would spare you for a couple of weeks. If you could read the serial and get fully up to date on it, and if I can get the authorisation, could you get down here immediately?"

"No problems, sir. Once I've got the okay, I will pick up the appropriate paperwork and be with you soon as."

Having authorised the secondment of his chosen coroner's officer, Woodall continued to keep in contact with those at the scene, whilst informing other essential parties of the progress of the enquiry.

The wide thorough search of both the building and the grounds started to reap rewards, and the exhibits officer was now continually recording and bagging possible court exhibits. During a further comprehensive search of the kitchen, a mat was moved and a locked cylindrical combination safe was discovered within the cement floor. Having no knowledge of the combination, a further search was carried out for its back-up key, which was located on the keys to both vehicles belonging to the brothers. On opening the safe, seven thousand pounds in large denomination bank notes were found inside; together with small, clear plastic packets of white powder (which officers thought to be cocaine), and a black velvet bag containing what the finders described as appearing to be expensive-looking female jewellery.

Following the discovery of the bodies, the exterior of the grounds was now under further scrutiny from the members of the search team, assisted by the K9 and handler. Not long into the search of a small young plantation, on rough ground distant from the cottage, the specialist search dog indicated an interest in the earth surrounding a small sapling supported by a wooden stake, with a red-painted top. On closer examination by the dog's handler, the sapling was found to be made of plastic. This caused officers to remove the stake and the replica sapling so as to dig up the earth beneath them. Having excavated only inches into the soil, a contact was made with the lid of a metal box. Once extracted, the unlocked box was found to contain gold Krugerrand coins and numerous items of women's jewellery. This discovery caused close examination of all of the remaining saplings in the plantation and two identical artificial trees were located. It was noted that similar to the red-topped stake, one had a white-painted top and the other blue. Beneath the soil in the plot marked with a white stake was found another metal box containing many items of male jewellery including Cartier and Rolex wristwatches. The soil below the blue stake appeared to have been recently disturbed and digging revealed a larger and narrower metal box, which when opened was found to be empty. All three excavated containers and the contents of two were then listed and allocated exhibit numbers.

Once aware of the seriousness of the possible charges that the Fergusons may face, DCI Byrne proceeded to make an application for authorisation that both men be detained in police custody for an extended period.

Now, with more than ample evidence, Woodall arranged for the initial interview to be carried out with each of the Ferguson brothers at the two separate police stations where they were held. To interview such hardened, life-long career criminals he chose his most experienced and seasoned crime fighters, DS Verna Cannan and DC Roger Buttle, both of whom had both been following every aspect of the case very closely. Before they commenced the tasks, Woodall imparted his own thoughts and suspicions to his trusted personnel. Both brothers had elected that their videotaped recorded interviews be carried out in the presence of solicitors, both from the same London-based company. Both accused had remained incommunicado at separate detention centres.

Later that evening, Woodall was speaking on the telephone to his colleague DCI Tony Byrne after he had received the news that both brothers, despite being shown the recovered items, had given entirely no comment interviews. This came as no surprise to either of the senior officers, considering the enormity of the possible charges.

It was decided to place personnel overnight at the scene to secure any further evidence that may come to notice during the continuing search the following day. Designated personnel were then contacted and informed of a briefing at Burgess Hill Police Station the following morning.

Later that evening, Woodall then made his weary way home.

Chapter 11
Bad to the Bone (1982)

Artist and Writer: George Thorogood

At 8:00 a.m. in an incident room at Burgess Hill Police Station, DCI Tony Byrne of the Major Crime Unit began the briefing of officers from his own team and others seconded to the operation. He led by very briefly running through the entire sequence of events, from the initial reports to the subsequent arrest of the Fergusons.

Following this he said, "This case will be managed by DI Woodall, whom most of you know. I will remain in the background on this one, because as many of you will know, I am retiring shortly and I need to get some urgent cases completed before I say my final farewells. He, with others, had an extremely long and successful day yesterday. So let's keep the momentum going and wrap this case up as soon and as efficiently as possible. Over to you, Jeff."

In response the DI replied, "Thanks for that, guv. I too would like to thank all who were involved yesterday. We got a lot done, but now comes the more difficult bit of tying it all together to get a conviction. Firstly, I would like to introduce the temporary members to the team. The office manager for this one is Sergeant David Williams, who brings his considerable experience from both the Force Operations Room and from similar investigations such as this. So he will be able to help with any queries whatsoever. Isn't that right, Dave?"

The quiet and unassuming sergeant smiled and briefly rose from his seated position replying, "I can't say I will have all the answers, but I will certainly try my best, sir."

The DI, with the aid of maps, photographs and written notes on the large whiteboards situated around the room, then gave a full, comprehensive verbal report of the incident, from the first alert when the shots were heard to have been fired, up to the present state of play. He included details of the Fergusons' previous history, and the fact that both had decided to give 'no comment' interviews.

After answering a number of queries, Woodall then said, "Our other temporary member is Sergeant Ramiz, who many of you will know, not only from his various policing roles, but also from his work with the Police Federation. He has kindly committed to act as coroner's officer and oversee all things concerning the two deceased, including the identification, the tracing of the relatives and, as it appears that they may both be foreign nationals, repatriation. He is well versed in such matters, so we couldn't have a better person for the job. Anything to add to that, Ram?"

"Blimey, I've now got to live up to that. Not really, sir. Only that if any new information comes in about either deceased, believed to be Stanescu and Gheata, please let me know as soon as possible, as it may be important not only from my side of things but also to the relatives or the coroner himself. Thank you."

After his comment DS Cannan raised her hand, and following an acknowledgement from Woodall commented, "It may not be at all connected, but a couple of years ago, this unit dealt with the murders of three men who were burnt to death after being locked in a porta cabin on a car wash site in Lewes. One of the dead was certainly named Stanescu, and he too worked in a similar occupation as this man of the same name. I wonder if they could be related?"

Byrne then interjected, "You're quite right, Verna. It was a case that we were both heavily involved with, which has remained undetected. I had also noticed the name, and I was going to speak to you after, it just may be a common name over the wider European community. However, it is odd that two men with that name and similar occupations have met violent deaths in the same county over a relatively short period of time. If I could allocate you the task of pulling that file and checking if there is any connection between the two? I would have liked to do this myself, but it looks as if I'm going to be tied up with the media for most of the day; especially as we will need to make some appeals for possible witnesses. Whatever the result, let myself and Sergeant Ramiz know."

The DS replied, "Will do, sir."

At the same time, PS Williams made a brief written note of the conversation, then after doing so, placed a copy of the task in a tray marked 'For Computer Entry.'

Woodall then commented, "We await that result with interest." He then introduced the senior crime scene investigator who related his team's current findings to date, including the retention of the burnt debris from the fire, which included the remnants of five shotgun cartridges. Two brushes' heads had also been seized, as it was suspected that at least one had brushed up what could possibly have been blood from the gravel drive close to the house. He further added that the Mondeo and pickup were in the process of being examined. He was hoping; although, there was little doubt that both of the deceased had used the Mondeo for their journey there, the fingerprints and DNA swabs that had been taken from them should prove positive occupation of the vehicle. With regard to the pickup, samples had been taken from the rear metal floor as it appeared that it had been washed, and early indications showed possible of traces of blood which were to be cross-matched with the blood of the two deceased. Work was proceeding in recovering bullets from the bodywork along the side of the vehicle. He explained that if a weapon was eventually found, there would be more than one bullet recovered for a comparison.

PS Duffell, the search team adviser was the next to comment. He spoke in detail of all findings by his unit, which included the two bodies and the floor safe together with its contents. He then went on to explain how the tops of three stakes coloured red, white and blue, amongst the many other plain wooden stakes, had been found to be the markers for buried suspected stolen goods.

On hearing this DC Kevin Reay stated excitedly, "I think that I've got it."

He momentarily paused to gather his thoughts as to how to address the audience about his matter in mind.

The DI interjected, "What have you got, Kev? If it's a dose of the clap, we can't help you here."

Laughing together with the entire assembly at Woodall's comment, the DC composed himself and replied, "No not this time, sir. After Gary and I had dealt with the abandoned Mondeo, as you instructed we collected all the paperwork from the house with a view to sifting through it today for anything of interest. Among various printed papers that were held by fridge magnets on a boiler inside a kitchen cupboard was a lone piece of notepaper. All that was handwritten in bold letters on this paper were the words 'Red', 'White' and 'Blue', and against each colour reference were some initials. I knew that it was a code for something, but at the time couldn't figure it out. It looks like this could well be connected to those identical coloured stakes."

"Can you remember what the initials were?"

"No, but I could easily put my hand on it as I submitted all the papers to Rick as possible exhibits."

Woodall's attention then turned to the seasoned exhibits officer, DC Rick Allard, a veteran of many similar enquiries.

"Rick, did you manage to find a safe place to house all the exhibits last night?"

Referring to an exhibit register resting on his knees, he replied, "I did, sir. They are all under lock and key in a large storage cupboard just along the corridor, and they include the paper that Kevin's referring to."

"Could you go with Kevin and fish it out, as this could be pertinent?"

As both officers rose from their chairs, DC Bye interjected, "Excuse me, guv, while they are going through those papers, it might be worth grabbing a supermarket delivery receipt that is amongst them. I found it laying on top of a plastic shopping bag filled with unopened bottles of booze. On reading the receipt it showed the bottles and other goods were delivered at 4:02 p.m. on the day before the shootings. It is possible that the delivery driver may have seen something that may be of interest."

After a short pause, Woodall responded, "Nice one, Gary, as by my calculations that delivery took place approximately only nine and a half hours prior to the shooting. It would be prudent to retrieve that receipt now while they are looking through the rest of the papers because, as you quite rightly say, that driver may have seen something helpful to the enquiry."

Turning his attention to the office manager, Woodall said, "Dave could make note of the fact that DC Bye is going to copy that receipt and task him to trace and speak to the delivery driver."

While awaiting the arrival of both papers, the DI spoke of the commencement of the search of the lake later that day by the underwater search unit, mentioning that such a probe, due to the expanse of water, would be their final opportunity to locate the missing automatic weapon within the Fergusons' property. The good news was that the divers had informed him that a preliminary inspection showed that as there were few branches overhanging the fairly shallow water, there appeared to be little silt on the lake bed, making for an easier search, and that their exploration was expected to be completed the following day.

On the return of officers, Allard and Reay, both Byrne and Woodall examined the retrieved papers. After their perusal of the receipt it was then handed to Bye, who signed the exhibits register, confirming that he was taking temporary possession of the paper exhibit.

While examining the paper referring to the three colours, Woodall addressed both search and exhibits officers, requesting them to confirm what property had been located under each separate coloured post.

Both confirmed that each hole contained a metal box. A total of 23 gold Krugerrand coins and assorted women's jewellery were buried under the red post. Found under the white post were a collection of male watches and jewellery. The bigger, recently disturbed hole indicated by the blue stake contained a larger empty metal box.

Then it was the DI's turn to show exuberance. "I've got it now," said Woodall.

Someone in the audience shouted, "Watch out everyone, it's catching."

Woodall then read out from the paper the initials written next to the word red, which were K + WJ, He then referred to the initials next to white which were W + MJ and the initial G next to the word blue.

"I have never been mistaken for a rocket scientist, but I believe that these initials represent the exact property that was found under each of the respective coloured stakes. This paper was a reminder to them which hole the items were in. I have a strong suspicion that G is for gun because there is a bigger container which is empty and it would appear that we have an automatic weapon outstanding."

There was a chuckle in the corner of the room.

Woodall said, "Come on, share the joke. What did I say that amused someone?"

The voice of Verna Cannan called out, "It wasn't you, sir. Someone who will remain nameless suggested G was for gerbil, as they like to burrow in the earth."

Woodall responded, "Tell whoever said that, Albourne is at present looking for a new village idiot and they've just passed their audition."

As distracting as such glib remarks and banter were, Woodall appreciated that such humour played a big part in uniting colleagues, both in the police and military when dealing with the most stressful and unpleasant of situations. So he tended to let such remarks pass without admonishment, unless they became tiresome or inappropriate.

"Okay. Returning to the serious business. As you all know, without any doubt there is an automatic weapon outstanding and this may help to confirm the fact, especially as all contents of the hole marked with the blue stake are missing and it has recently been disturbed. I would suggest that as the thorough search of the entire cottage and grounds has not revealed the gun, the weapon we are seeking could only be in the lake or removed by the mystery vehicle that was believed to leave the scene very shortly after the shooting was heard. I am hopeful that as the shotgun was hidden underwater in the boat house, the same will apply to the outstanding gun."

Woodall continued, "If this is the case or not, it now becomes a very important task to try to shed some light on this unknown vehicle, as the shell casing found indicate that the shots that hit the truck were fired from a completely different place from where Daniel Ferguson tells us that an unknown person fired from. When I asked him about the mystery vehicle and driver, he suggested it was the person who did the shooting, giving a completely different location. This lie indicates that the occupants of this vehicle are in some way heavily involved in what happened there. Both independent witnesses living opposite the property, categorically state that a vehicle of some sort exited that drive, without lights, very shortly after the sounds of shots fired. Neither witness actually saw it or can give its direction of travel."

He then moved across the room to a wall where a large map was displayed, and pointing to a specific location said, "Our best chance of tracing it is if it eventually joined the nearby A23, then if it travelled north or south it would hopefully be captured by one of the various traffic cameras. If it left the scene and went in the other direction towards the A281, then I doubt if there are any such cameras and we may have to rely on any images captured from private houses. That sounds like a big task, but the advantage that we have on this occasion is we know almost the exact time that it left, and presuming the driver is not hanging about gives us a possible timing to certain locations, as at that time of night traffic would be light."

Turning to Sergeant Williams, "David, following this briefing can you allocate this task?"

The sergeant nodded and began writing in his log.

DCI Byrne then spoke, "Thanks, Jeff. I think you have covered most of what we know so far. Any questions?"

DC Dave Mills raised his hand, and after acknowledgment from Byrne, said, "Have we got any idea of why this all kicked off?"

Byrne replied, "Because of both of the Fergusons' lifetime involvement in crime, there could be numerous scenarios. It could be gangland enemies, someone that they had crossed, or simply revenge. We can't even rule out attempted robbery, due to the amount of money and valuables found there. I am led to believe from some in the know about such things, that all the jewellery found is of very high quality, and the Krugerrands alone are valued at over £20,000. Who is carrying out the searches on the recovered property?"

P.C Hands, a local intelligence officer, who due to his vast experience and local knowledge was often called upon to assist in similar major operations, raised his arm stating, "That will be me, sir."

"How's it going, Ian, has any of it been identified yet?"

"It's not been confirmed yet sir, and I didn't want to mention it before being 100% certain, because we could have egg on our face if it gets out and it's not what it appears to be. But as you have asked, it is looking like most, if not all, of the seized jewellery and gold coins are part of the burglary that took place in April 2015 at the Hatton Garden underground safe deposit company."

Woodall responded, "Wow! When did you find this out?"

"I circulated the descriptions and photos of some of it over a wide force area yesterday afternoon, and this morning just before briefing I had a message to that effect. An officer from the Met, who was involved in the original investigation, is fairly positive that he recognises a couple of rare pieces and is now searching records for all of the outstanding property from the job. Apparently, estimates are that from the 14 million pounds of valuables stolen, there is still over ten million outstanding."

"Okay. Firstly, well done Ian, for recognising the fact that if this is so, we need to keep it under our hats until it's confirmed."

Addressing the entire room, the DI firmly stated, "I don't want a word of this possible connection between our job and the Hatton Garden one leaving this room, even though several were arrested and jailed for that raid; I believe that some others responsible remain at large. The Fergusons could have been involved, but knowing a bit about the case I wouldn't think so. I think it's more likely that these two Herberts have possibly considered that they've got a bit too long in the tooth for hard graft like robbery, so instead, from their ill-gotten gains they have purchased a place in the sticks to fence nicked gear for all their villainous mates. The other reason is, if the press gets a whiff, we will be further inundated with even more enquiries than we are receiving now, and there is no certainty yet regarding the connection with our recovered property. If this does leak out before the official confirmation, heads will roll. Everyone understand?"

The whole room indicated to comply with his instruction.

The scenes of crime officer then interjected, "We will need to have a look at it all before it gets handled too much, as if it is from the Hatton Garden burglary anything found could implicate not only the two in custody but also further offenders. It now becomes imperative for us to examine it quickly as the Met will be asking if we have done so."

P.C Hands then added, "The buried property and that recovered from the floor safe is all bagged and labelled in the exhibit cupboard, ready when required."

The scene examiner replied, "Ian, I will see you immediately following this briefing."

Woodall then address all assembled saying, "We are building a good case against these two, who need to be put away for a long time, but there's still plenty to get on with. If you haven't been allocated a task yet, make yourself known to Sergeant Williams, as I'm sure he has plenty that have not yet been allocated."

As the enquiry team slowly departed from the room, both Woodall and Byrne continued in their roles of overseeing the entire investigation.

It was about midday when news from the completed tasks started to come into the incident desk. The results and generated paperwork from each enquiry were then examined by the office manager, who following his required action, would then pass it to the Holmes (Home Office Large Major Enquiry System) team for permanent computerised recording.

Once the crime scene officers had examined all of the recovered valuables, the full descriptions and the photographs were forwarded to the relevant Metropolitan Police office. After their close examination, the conclusion was that most were part of the Hatton Garden haul.

Both Byrne and Woodall realised that this discovery would take the enquiry in a further direction. Being such a high-profile case, it would automatically trigger the involvement of another force, not only to continue to further investigate what had been described as the largest burglary in England's legal history, but they would also wish to obtain as much information regarding London's criminal underworld from two of its former long-term gang members. The two senior officers were adamant that such enquiries would have to wait and could not at that moment cause any distraction from the possible murder enquiry. Both felt sure that if eventually charged with serious offences, within time, both the brothers would be attempting to strike some form of a deal to lessen their sentences by giving vital information about the criminal underworld with which they were so familiar.

Their discussion was soon followed by contact from DC Bye, who reported that he had traced the supermarket delivery driver and had obtained a written statement from him. The witness could remember delivering to the

Fergusons' address on the afternoon prior to the incident. He initially stated that he had visited the property on numerous occasions before and could not recollect seeing anything particularly unusual on the day in question. When asked what vehicles had been present during his visit, he mentioned the blue pickup and the mustang, both of which he had seen in past visits. The mention of vehicles then reminded him that on that particular afternoon there had been a medium size white motor home parked at the rear of the cottage, which he had never seen there before. He had taken a brief interest in the vehicle as he was considering purchasing something similar in the near future, but from his cab he could not establish the make or model as there were no markings or emblems visible from his position. He even attempted to look at the registration plates to establish the year of manufacture, but both registration plates were obstructed by large refuse bins and outdoor furniture. He did notice that it was hooked up to an external electricity plug fixed to the cottage, and he thought that it could either belong to one of the anglers, he had passed by at the lake or the Fergusons had visitors. It did cross his mind to enquire about it, in case whoever owned it was considering selling it, but because of the surly demeanour of the bald-headed occupant who received the goods, he decided not to do so and left the premises without speaking to anyone further.

Following no further notable developments, once officers had completed their allocated tasks the incident room was closed for the night.

On his way home Woodall drove to Lakeside Cottage and spoke to the two officers who were guarding the scene for a second night. As a constable he had been selected for equally mundane duties. Suspecting that they were about to experience a long twelve-hour shift with little incentive, he reminded both that there was always the possibility that some of the Fergusons' criminal associates, knowing that they were now incarcerated, may visit to retrieve stolen property that they thought may be still be on the premises, or to recover any incriminating evidence, bearing in mind a gun was still unaccounted for. Woodall, although, not suspecting intruders was sure that having implanted such thoughts in their heads, they would now remain fully vigilant over their entire shift. Such a thought-provoking scenario would have certainly motivated himself to remain alert had he been in their position.

Chapter 12
I Fought the Law (1979)

Artists: The Clash
Writer: Sonny Curtis

The following morning's briefing began reflecting on the results of the previous day's enquiries. Following this, the DI gave a brief resume regarding the unidentified vehicle that the delivery driver had seen only hours prior to the incident.

This prompted him to say, "For those who don't know him, let me introduce you to a local officer, PC Richard Shunter, who knows the area extremely well and, knowing him as I do, has probably run around most of it all numerous times. Over to you, Dick."

Shunter stood and responded, "Thanks, sir. As the governor said, together with other divisional officers we carried out house-to-house calls on the few houses within earshot, or should I say gunshot, of Lakeside Cottage. We gained no further useful information, although, some householders did hear some muffled shots in the distance but presumed it was night-time poachers, which is not that uncommon out there. As there were so few farms and houses to call on, we were then given the task of carrying out the CCTV enquiry."

He then approached the large map, and while indicating various locations, said to the gathering, "The task was to attempt to find a direction of travel of the unknown vehicle that left the scene soon after the shooting, and I think we may have a result. It could have been a lot better, but it does possibly confirm what the delivery driver saw."

As he continued speaking, the atmosphere in the room became palpable.

"As we knew the approximate time it left the drive was 1:45, we were able to check a number of cameras on both carriageways of the A23 between Crawley and Brighton during the relevant time scales. This search was relatively easy because, as expected, traffic was light and the only suspect vehicle suggested was the white camper type van, which would seldom be seen travelling at that time of night. As we saw no sign of any similar vehicle from these cameras at the relevant times, we switched our efforts to look for a similar vehicle travelling westbound from the scene. As this route is mainly country roads it proved far more difficult to locate any cameras covering the roads. We called at numerous possible premises situated close to the roadside which may have had some CCTV coverage of the westbound carriage way of the A281. Nothing came to our notice until we reached the Shell garage on the southern end of Henfield village."

The officer again paused and, pointing at a specific location on the map, he then continued, "This business is situated on the west side of a mini-roundabout at the junction of the A281 and the A2037 which has cameras covering the petrol pumps. One of the cameras, as well as scanning some of the pumps, also includes a small section of the road at the mini-roundabout in the High Street. On examining the footage of this camera during the morning in question, at 1:51 a.m. the wheels and lower part of what appears similar to the bodywork of a camper van turned right from the A281 onto the roundabout and continued to travel northwards onto the High Street. If the camera had been set slightly higher it could have captured the index number, but as we all know it rarely works out like that." His comment was met with wry smiles and much head nodding.

He continued, "Having now timed myself driving from the scene to the garage, the time of travel was spot on. The camera showed little other traffic between the relevant times, so I would suggest that there is a very strong possibility this was our vehicle. Having examined the film several times, unless someone had specific knowledge of such motors, there are no markings or damage whatsoever to help identify it. I am in the process of circulating the stills to garages that specialise in such transport in an effort to at least establish the make and model. Following this discovery, the team then checked out all business premises in the High Street for any useful CCTV coverage, but without a result. The A281 then runs on for twelve miles before it reaches the next town of Horsham, and there are many junctions before reaching there. We concluded the search in Henfield and await instruction on whether to resume the enquiry further north. What is interesting, I would suggest the driver of that vehicle may have little local knowledge, because if he had intended to travel straight through Henfield, there was a shorter and less obvious country route he could have taken. Although, at that time of night, the driver may have considered the main road was a faster route to put miles between themselves and the scene."

Woodall responded, "Thanks for that, Richard. We will await any news of what type of vehicle that was, and if identified we can plan the next course of action."

Shortly following the briefing, Woodall received some very positive news from the underwater search unit, to the effect that they had started locating submerged items. Woodall enthusiastically contacted the exhibits officer DC Allard, requesting him to secure the necessary exhibit kit and join him in his vehicle. Having made their way to the lake, they were spoken to by police diver PC Jonathan Lelliott, who immediately pointed to three very wet and muddy sub-machine guns, now laying on the bank of the lake, together with a number of spent bullet cases. The officer explained that all three weapons and shells had been found, spread out in a relatively small area in throwing distance from the water's edge closest to the cottage. He added that due to the close proximity of the discarded items, it gave the impression that they had all been discarded from the same place at the same time.

All of the officers present were equally surprised, and at the same time elevated at the discovery, with the realisation that they had recovered not the one weapon that they hoped for but three. Although, initially confusing, this indicated that the two deceased were also possibly armed and following their deaths all three weapons and the ejected shells had been disposed of in the water by one of the Fergusons. The DI considered that such finds would possibly give them ample evidence to implicate the brothers in the deaths of Stanescu and Gheata.

With gloved hands, DC Allard carefully bagged all three weapons and the recovered shell casings for the preservation of any evidence and for the eventual transportation to the crime scene office. He then requested the diver who located the gun to sign the appropriate exhibit label. On the suggestion of Woodall, he, together with Allard and Lelliott, walked to the nearby plantation, and on locating the blue stake from where the larger metal box had been excavated, each bagged gun was placed in turn beside the relevant burrow and photographed, confirming that any of the three weapons could have been concealed there. The officers discussed that an internal forensic examination of the box may have established which firearm had been stored inside, but due to their submersion in the lake it was thought that such a result was now highly unlikely. However, the bullets recovered from the pickup and the body of Stanescu would identify the weapon responsible.

Once the entire lake had been searched and no further property found, Woodall called all of the search officers together to establish if they were entirely satisfied that nothing else could be hidden there. When told that both the land and water searches were complete to the satisfaction of all involved; he thanked all for their diligent and successful work.

On returning to the incident room, Woodall made contact with all officers involved with the case, requesting that on the completion of their present enquiries they return and see him. It was now essential that having gained sufficient evidence, he scaled down the operation to release detectives to assist in other current cases and to investigate reports of further serious crimes which he knew would be imminent. During the afternoon and evening, the teams returned at different intervals and after handing their completed enquiries to the office manager they were then spoken to by Woodall. He informed them that as the search of the scene was complete, once officers had finalised their allotted tasks the incident room would be manned by the case officers only, who would prepare the prosecution file against the Fergusons. He thanked all those who had been seconded to the operation and who would not be returning the following day.

Two days after the decision was taken to wind down the investigation, DCI Byrne was sitting in his office busily examining various documents when DS Cannan knocked on his closed door. After acknowledgement, she entered, and after the usual pleasantries said in an invigorating manner, "Sir, as you will obviously remember, at the start of the Ferguson enquiry you gave me the task of looking at any link between Ivan Stanescu who died in the fire at the car wash about two years ago, and one of the latest shooting victims, Yannis Stanescu. I can now say, with certainty, they were brothers. From immigration records it appears that Yannis, the younger of the two, came to this country shortly after the death of Ivan, stayed and took over exactly the same position that his brother once held in the car wash company."

Byrne, who was taking great interest in this news, straightened himself in his chair saying, "That's what you call jumping into dead man's shoes. A bit rich though when it's your brother. I have known you for a long time, Verna. I can tell by your demeanour that you've got something even more interesting to come."

Smiling, she replied, "Well it's funny you should say that. This morning I received the records back from the telephone investigation unit on the most recent calls made and received by both Gheata's and Stanescu's mobile phones which were found in the hire car. I have been examining both of them with the crime analyst. It doesn't appear at this stage that there is anything of particular interest on Gheata's phone records for us, although, obviously as they come from the Met area we will pass both records to them, as they may have other intelligence that we don't know of. Now, we come to the interesting bit: Two days before he was shot, the phone belonging to Stanescu received a very interesting two-minute call from an address in Brighton."

"Come on, Verna, spit it out. Where's this leading to?"

"Does Cowley Drive, Woodingdean ring any bells?"

Open-mouthed Byrne replied, "You're joking. That's the road where Mrs French was staying with her parents after she was raped, and we suspected that her husband killed the five men who were in some way involved, which included Ivan Stanescu. Was the call made from their house?"

"No, it wasn't, but by the house number of the property from which the call was made, it would appear that it's situated close by. It may be just coincidental, but unlikely because as you know, most of the buildings on that part of the road are bungalows, many occupied by elderly residents who are extremely unlikely to communicate with the likes of Stanescu. The number comes down to a Donald McKinnon. The call was made by a landline and an enquiry with his provider reveals that this phone is due to be cut off very shortly for non-payment of his bill. I also carried out a voters' register check and it shows him living alone at the address. A PNC check shows only a drink-driving conviction, no other criminal convictions."

"This is interesting. You don't think the husband of Mrs French is now shacked up with this McKinnon character, and for some reason which, I cannot think of, has contacted Ivan's brother?"

"It just doesn't make any sense. Why would French, if he did kill Ivan want to contact Yannis, who as far as we are aware wasn't even in the country when Mrs French was raped? I'm pretty sure it wouldn't be to say sorry for killing his brother."

Byrne responded jovially, "An apology does seem highly unlikely and would probably not be very well received. It may just be an amazing coincidence, but we'd better get an enquiry done there soon. Let Jeff know all of this, because as much as I would like to once again be involved in the French case, I shall soon be putting my feet up and hopefully doing a bit of world travel, and I can't say that I would relish the idea of having to return for a court case."

After informing Woodall of the development, the following day DS Cannan, together with another detective from her unit, called at the address of Donald McKinnon. On their arrival at the address, she immediately noticed that the property was situated almost opposite the bungalow where Melanie French had once been living. Having no response from their repeated knocking at the door, it soon became obvious that McKinnon's address was unoccupied. There were no curtains or blinds at any of the windows and on peering through the grimy glass, the officers could see that the entire premises were in complete disarray. On the tops of the sparse furniture, documents relating to final demands for payment were clearly visible. The entire interior appeared shabby and floors were littered with empty alcohol bottles and food wrappers. The bedclothes, on one bed present, gave the impression that they had not been changed for a considerable time.

In an effort so as not to alert either McKinnon or Melanie French or her family as to their real interest, both officers called at the addresses of the immediate neighbours, purporting to be investigating bogus callers who had been active in the area. During these proceedings they were able to confirm that two days before, bailiffs had arrived and evicted McKinnon, who was last seen walking off carrying just two bags. Neither of the neighbours had seen anyone else either regularly visiting or staying there since his wife had left him. When asked where he may have gone to, they explained that due to his drinking and volatile nature, nobody in the road spoke to him and he made no effort to change the situation. It was established that he was a regular customer at the nearby supermarket, where he regularly purchased alcohol.

Under the same pretence, the officers called at the address of Melanie's parents, and having not received a reply were informed by the next-door neighbour that they were on holiday with their daughter. Knowing that Melanie was the only sibling, this confirmed to Cannan that she had returned from Venezuela. This led the detective to further consider the present whereabouts of her illusive husband, Dennis French.

The detectives then turned their investigation to the nearby supermarket where McKinnon was well known to most members of the staff, as he was once employed there until he was dismissed due to his drinking and bad timekeeping. They learnt that until recently he had been a daily visitor to purchase alcohol, and that on occasions when he was short of money he would try to obtain credit, but as it was never allowed he could become abusive. One of the staff had recently had a conversation with him, when he mentioned going back to Scotland but had not named a precise area.

Extensive enquiries were then carried out in an effort to trace McKinnon to establish his relationship with Yannis Stanescu. The majority of the investigation was centred on his possible connections in Scotland. But despite numerous communications with the obvious organisations, such as job centres and council departments, the whereabouts of McKinnon remained a mystery to the investigation team. This result was of no surprise, as someone being chased for so many debts was always going to be difficult to locate. However, all involved were certain that at some stage it would be necessary for him to seek financial help or housing benefits, and when he did so DS Cannan was positive that given time the team's persistent searches would reap the reward.

With the majority of the evidence gathered, both Michael and Barry Ferguson were again interviewed in an identical manner as before. However, on this occasion, when confronted with the mass of evidence put before them and their solicitors, they confessed to shooting Stanescu and Gheata, handling stolen property, firearms offences and possession of a class 'A' drug, along with the further offences of attempting to conceal the bodies.

During the interview, in mitigation both stated that the entire incident had initiated when less than two days earlier they received an anonymous telephone call. The content of the conversation with the unknown caller was such that it caused them to recover the hidden guns to protect themselves against an imminent attack from the alleged armed intruders. The information proved to be correct and they shot both men to protect themselves. They planned to transport the bodies away from their property to another location where they could be found quickly and not connected to them, but on seeing the traffic car, they panicked and put the corpses into the sewer pit. Daniel admitted disposing of the three guns and the spent ammunition in the lake, while Michael had placed the shotgun under the boat in the boathouse and then burnt the used ammunition, together with the clothing that they had both been wearing, as he thought the cartridges would float. Both insisted that all of the identified stolen property of Krugerrands, jewellery, guns and drugs were purchased on different occasions, from the same person at a notorious East London pub. When asked about the broken windows in their conservatory and the two pebbles that appeared to have been responsible, Daniel Ferguson truthfully claimed that he had not seen the damage, as he had not entered that part of the building since the incident. Michael stated that he thought the person he had shot must have thrown them to entice him out of the building. He was informed that his theory may be correct, and both pebbles found inside the conservatory had been forensically examined but no evidence was obtained from either to establish how, or who had been responsible for projecting them there.

Both brothers, apparently for their own safety, would not disclose from whom they had received the identified stolen property or the source of the firearms and ammunition. Both were then charged with the numerous offences disclosed and remanded in custody by local magistrates to stand trial at a later date. After the charges were made, the interviewing officers DS Cannan and DC Buttle, informed DI Woodall of the successful result.

DC Buttle said to Woodall, "Even though the charges were so serious, confronted with the mountain of evidence, those two tough guys realised that they needed to give some form of explanation, or they could be convicted as cold-blooded murderers. Their explanations were remarkably consistent, bearing in mind that they have had no communication with each other since the time of their arrest, so for once in their lives the majority of what they have both said could possibly be true. Their version of events may help to explain at least some of what happened there that night. What is interesting, and in some way may verify their account of events, is that a telephone enquiry with their landline provider shows that at the time and date they say they received the apparent warning, records show that there was an incoming call from an unidentified phone. Obviously they could be lying about the content of the call, but there is little doubt that Stanescu and Gheata hired a car for one day only, drove from London to Sussex at night, and hid the vehicle in trees close to the attacked premises. They then left the contents of their pockets in the hire car, presumably so as to make a silent approach, and both it appears were in possession of sub-machine guns. If the Fergusons are to be believed, if they hadn't received the supposed warning then they would have both been in bed and at the mercy of the two intruders, but instead were armed and ready for them. This explanation does make sense.

"The only inconsistency is this business with the camper van. Michael Ferguson only admitted its presence when told it was seen by a witness, and then he excused his initial denial by saying it had slipped his mind and it was a mate of theirs who called in for a couple of hours and left before the intruders arrived. Of course, he won't name his mate as he says that he doesn't want to get him involved. When its presence was first mentioned to Daniel, he initially used that vehicle as an excuse of its occupants causing the bullet holes in their truck, but he has now admitted that he fired the shots that killed Stanescu and which caused the damage. He is now denying seeing the motorhome at all, saying it must have been an angler getting a crafty top-up of electricity while they were out. We know this is not true, because the delivery driver saw the motorhome at the premises when he delivered the goods to someone who fits the description of Michael Ferguson. Both are obviously lying about this one particular aspect, which tends to suggest that this vehicle in some way has a large part to play in connection with this incident."

DS Cannan then continued, "If both witnesses are correct and a vehicle did leave the scene just after the shootings, as they said the engine sounded bigger than the average car then it could well have been that motorhome. The fact that it left without lights shows at the very least some guilty knowledge, but I can't think what part, if any, the occupant or occupants played in this, as the Fergusons have admitted all of the offences. They have now been charged and remanded in custody until their crown court appearance, and the world will be a far safer place for hopefully a long time."

DC Buttle then commented, "Returning to the subject of the Fergusons landline activity. This number received a call at 1:29 a.m. which was about the time that it was all kicking off. The call, which was answered lasted only ten seconds, and it is not surprising knowing the circles that they mix in was made from a Burnaphone. When asked about this call both brothers have denied receiving it, which again indicates that it is somehow relevant to the incident. We know that neither of the deceased made it, so could it have been another warning regarding the imminent attack, or even from the unknown occupant of the camper van. Dick Shunter has managed to get the vehicle that was partially caught by the garage CCTV camera identified as possibly an Elddis Autoquest Motorhome, but of course there is no certainty that this is the one that we are looking for, as there could have been a similar vehicle on that road at that time, but it's got to be a good bet. Although, the witnesses can't say in which direction the vehicle went, Dick is quite right to say that if this is the one we are looking for, by passing the garage it must have turned left out of the drive. If it had made a right-hand turn, it could have reached the northern end of Henfield by a shorter, quieter country route. This would tend to suggest that the driver was not local, or for some reason wanted to go into the village itself."

Woodall then said, "That's interesting. We've pretty much tied up this job but for the two mysterious phone calls and the identity of this camper van, which throws up many questions. Was the driver from out of the area, or just unaware of the shorter route, or did he want for some reason to enter the village? Can you both make arrangements to get the description of this vehicle circulated to local units and to get the streets of Henfield checked out at night, when most vehicles are parked up, to see if a similar vehicle can be located? It's a long shot but we have nothing else to go on. If we are able to trace it, we may get the answers to those two telephone calls."

Cannan then said, "I hate to throw a spanner in the works, and you may think I've lost my senses, but could Melanie French's husband Dennis be the occupant of that motorhome? We ought to consider this, as we suspect that French killed, amongst others, Ivan Stanescu for being in possession of a video film of the rape of his wife. We are now dealing with the death of his brother, Yannis Stanescu, who has been shot dead by Daniel Ferguson, and who less than two days before this killing received a telephone call warning of the attack. This anonymous call originated from a property situated opposite where Melanie was staying with

179

her parents after being raped. Of course, it may be a coincidence, but it is most odd."

Woodall: "If we were to consider that, then French would have to have some connection to the Fergusons. Is that likely?"

Cannan: "No, it's not. Despite the horrendous offences that we suspect French may have committed, it would be most unlikely for him to associate with the likes of them. He has no criminal convictions and our previous enquiries showed him as a retired first-class soldier and a normal every day, honest and hard-working citizen."

Woodall: "Have the Fergusons got any military experience? Could he know either from that?"

Buttle: "Definitely not, sir. I've studied both of their antecedent history. Neither has ever had legit work and they've been in and out of prison for most of their lives."

Woodall: "In reality, even if the CCTV had captured the registration number of the camper and we were to trace it, at this stage we have no way of connecting it to the scene. There are no fingerprints or footprints for comparison to any possible occupant and as it was parked on a concrete base there were no tyre tread impressions left behind. Until we have any other suspects as to the driver of that camper, it would do no harm in looking to see if French has returned to the UK. When you have organised the search for the camper in Henfield, could you contact the immigration authorities to see if French has come back? If he has, then we need to speak with him about this as well as the original job."

Chapter 13
I'm Moving On (2001)

Artists: Rascal Flatts
Writers: Phillip White, D. Vincent Williams

After a long untroubled sleep, Dutch switched on the transistor radio that had previously served him so well and listened to the local radio station for any news of the shootings. Later he was able to read the Brighton Evening Argus, but neither told him any more than that the police were dealing with what was described as a serious incident near the village of Albourne. After a lengthy telephone conversation with his wife, and informing her that he now considered it safe for her and her parents to return home, he shaved off his now lengthy beard and asked Jeanette to return what he considered was long hair back to his normal much shorter style.

During his time at Jeanette's and awaiting Melanie's return, he contacted his brother Roy, who as a child he had once been very close to, but apart from the odd telephone conversation they had not seen each other since their grandfather's funeral. Dennis and Roy, with their brother Barry and two sisters, had lived with their grandparents following the death of their soldier father whilst serving in Northern Ireland and their mother's subsequent suicide. The elderly grandparents had found it both physically and financially difficult to manage a family of seven, especially as all of the children, because of their disadvantaged lifestyle, were the subject of severe and constant bullying. When, at the age of ten, Dennis and Roy, were caught stealing fruit from a Brighton market stall that, together with an accumulation of other domestic problems, caused the local social services department to intervene. Due to such recurring problems, the siblings were parted by the authorities and cared for by other family members. Dennis went to live with his aunt and uncle and their two sons in Denmead, Hampshire, while his half-sister and half-brother Deborah and Barry moved to their parental mother's home near Swindon, leaving Sister Jeanette to remain at the home of the grandparents and Roy to continue to reside with other relatives within Brighton. Although, Dennis had been extremely happy living with his loving grandparents, life at his new home was less chaotic and where he was able to gain more self-confidence, improve his education and become very proficient at all sports, especially middle-distance running. All of these characteristics made him an excellent candidate to follow in the footsteps of his father and join the regular army at the age of sixteen, where he immediately qualified as a paratrooper and was given the nickname of Dutch by his colleagues, who thought it apt to change his surname to another nationality.

Meeting at a city centre pub, the brothers soon began lengthy conversations, predominately reminiscing about their various youthful exploits and combined admiration of their grandparents for their unwavering attempts to keep the family together with very little funds or additional assistance. Dutch mentioned their discovery of the nuclear fall-out post that he had recently visited. Roy's response to the memory showed how different they now were, as Roy's immediate thoughts were to the effect that it was unfortunate that the shelter did not have mains facilities, as it would make an excellent clandestine cannabis growing facility. During their time together, Roy expressed sympathy for Melanie's past ordeal, at the same time attempting to prise information from Dutch as to his possible involvement in the deaths of Melanie's tormentors. Dutch put him in no doubt that he did not wish to discuss the matter, which may soon be subject to intense police scrutiny. Roy, who had continued to have regular brushes with the law, did not fully understand why his brother would not indulge in that particular conversation but respected his wishes.

Dutch, knowing of Roy's past, asked him who he considered was the best criminal defence solicitor in the city. After very little thought Roy recommended Tim Hunt, a name that Dutch considered would be easy to remember for very possible future reference. Before their departure the brothers agreed that they, together with Jeanette, would visit both their sister and brother, Deborah and Barry, from whom they had been split up since childhood, both of whom had remained living in the Swindon area.

With the welcome return of Melanie and her parents, Dutch arranged to meet his wife at his temporary accommodation at Jeanette's home, as he did not wish any of the neighbours, especially Nesbitt, to see him visiting Cowley Drive.

Shortly into their emotional reunion, Dutch sensed he could detect that Melanie was wanting to ask him something but wasn't quite sure how to approach the subject. Suspecting what was concerning her he said, "If you are wondering as to what's happened about the possible threat towards us, it's been sorted."

"Are you sure? I've been too worried to ask, as we have my mum and dad to think about as well."

"I'm sure and will be even more confident once we've moved."

"Dare I ask how you can be so certain?"

"The two blokes that you saw are no longer around to be a threat."

In a raised, anxious voice Melanie replied, "Oh, for Christ's sake, Dennis! I do hope that doesn't mean you've done something stupid, yet again. Surely we already have enough to worry about?"

In an attempt to calm his agitated wife, he replied in a quiet manner, "I can assure you that; although, I have been partly responsible for eliminating the threat, I did not physically take part. Something had to be done for us all to continue our lives in a normal safe manner, so I took the best option in which I was not directly involved. Let's just leave the matter there and get on with our lives and hopefully a new peaceful future. You know fully well why I can't tell you anymore."

Melanie could tell from his tone that the matter was no longer up for discussion. She was aware that his reasoning for not telling her more was so as not to cause her to lie to the police or anyone else on his behalf. Although, curious, she was in agreement with him that due to the possible circumstances, the least she knew the better.

Melanie was, however, certain that any actions he had taken against the threat would have been carried out for the protection of both her and her family. The reunited couple then engaged in a very long meaningful conversation regarding their future together, which very much depended on his fate. He could choose to attempt to live an anonymous life in another part of the country and hope that he would never come to the notice of the police, but he did not envy the thought of regularly misleading people regarding his past and the continual need to be constantly looking over his shoulder. The only other option was to take the risk and give himself up, in the hope that the police had found no further evidence to connect him to either of the fatal incidents; if this proved to be the case then he would be able to continue the rest of his life without concern for his wife or himself. They both agreed that whatever his eventual decision was to be, they would in conjunction with Melanie's parents begin immediate planning for their move to the Lake District for a new, and in Dutch's case anonymous, start in an isolated part of Cumbria far away from Melanie's painful memories.

During their long conversation Melanie happened to mention that the neighbours had informed her that the police had called at her parents' bungalow. As she said the words, Dutch's heart skipped a beat but was instantly relieved when she continued to say that they were making enquiries into bogus callers in the area. However, he did wonder in the back of his mind if they had in some way been alerted of his return from Venezuela. Such worrying thoughts would make him extra careful while remaining in Brighton.

Having talked through the possible scenarios, Melanie produced numerous brochures issued by various Cumbrian-based estate agents, which Dutch examined enthusiastically. He made known his preferences, but as his immediate future was far from being certain he decided that the final choice of a house and its location should lay with Melanie and her parents. At the same time he hoped above all else that he had a future with them, which was dependent on if he had covered his tracks efficiently enough so as not to have left any damning evidence at either Devil's Dyke or the Lewes car wash. He remained confident that he could not be connected to the incident at the fishery.

With both properties being mortgage free, preparations to relocate were made by both couples. Melanie's parents placed their bungalow on the property market, while Melanie gave the required notice of their intention to sell the premises to the tenants of their flat at Goldstone Court, Hove. Once the flat was vacant, Melanie, again alone dealt with its sale as their intention was for the time being, to keep the name of Dennis French as anonymous as possible.

Whilst, waiting for these transactions to take place, Jeanette was more than happy to have her brother staying with her. To show his gratitude, Dutch shared the chores, carried out DIY and paid rent. He further promised that once they were settled she would always be welcome to stay with them in Cumbria whenever she wanted a holiday.

As Dutch did not feel that it was prudent to visit Cowley Drive, he would meet Melanie, together with her parents, Ken and Molly, to discuss all of their future plans at various locations. It was at one of these meetings that it was decided that the best way forward was to pool all of the capital raised from both the bungalow and the flat, which together would be sufficient to make a cash purchase of one of the very desirable properties that they had chosen in Cumbria. Ken and Molly were in their late sixties, and although fit and well for their ages were far too advanced in years to obtain a mortgage. As the flat was jointly owned, Dutch had to sign the necessary sale papers, but they were confident that there was no reason for such documents to come to the attention of the police. In order that Dutch could remain anonymous in the transaction, the new property would be purchased solely by Ken and Molly, who would then bequeath it in their wills to their only child, Melanie. All agreed that this proposal was the best solution to the current situation in which Dutch found himself.

It was during one of her regular visits to Chapel Street that Melanie informed Dutch that Nesbitt had been evicted from his home by bailiffs. All of his belongings had since been removed, leaving the bungalow vacant. This was pleasing news for Dutch, as Nesbitt was the only person who could connect him to the Fergusons' address, but as risky as it was, it was a chance he had to take; being the one and only method of enticing their tormentors into his trap. Before taking this risk he had considered that even if the brief meeting with Nesbitt came to the notice of the police, he hoped that he had taken enough steps, to make it unlikely that he could positively identify him, because at that time Dutch had longer hair, a beard, and was also wearing glasses and a beanie hat. He also thought it was unlikely, because even though Nesbitt saw him leave his in-laws' home, he appeared to be partially drunk and may not still remember the address mentioned when Dutch purportedly called for a taxi, but even if he did it was only circumstantial evidence, providing no proof of him being involved in the killings.

Once the sales of both properties had been agreed, the couples travelled together to the Lake District to view their short list of a potential home for them all. It took only a short time for them to agree on a country-style cottage with an annexe near the small town of Ambleside.

Both couples volunteered to live in the annexe, but Molly and Ken insisted that they would reside there, as due to their advancing years they would appreciate the less work involved living in the smaller residence. The elderly couple did not resent moving home for the continuing safety of their daughter, as they both agreed that, as reckless as they suspected that their son-in-law's actions had been, they too had harboured a burning desire for some form of justice to be taken against the perpetrators of the horrific attack on their daughter, that would haunt both them and their daughter forever.

The move proceeded quickly without any major complications. As the cottage had been well maintained and newly decorated, there was little work required to make it the perfect home for both couples. Once settled, Dutch decided it was time to regain some of the fitness that he had lost over the years, when he only had a treadmill to run on because it had not been safe to run outside of the Venezuelan compound. Now, running mile after mile in such beautiful unspoilt countryside, sometimes with Jodie, made him feel like his old self, before the tragic attack on Melanie. Following her traumatic ordeal on the Sussex Downs, she never thought that she would ever walk the dog alone again, but since moving she had been doing so, though in more populated areas. With her previous qualifications and together with an excellent reference from Mr Chamberlain, her previous employer in Venezuela, Melanie had been able to secure employment at a local play school. Dutch was now confident that they could get their old lives back together with this new start, but such contented feelings were constantly disrupted with the awareness that he would always be wanted by the police. Dutch knew that sooner or later, no matter where he lived in the UK, he would eventually come to the notice of the police and be arrested, or he could voluntarily give himself up on his own terms and hope for the best outcome.

Although, they were all financially sound and enjoying their new lifestyles together, he was aware that he would need to obtain work, not only for financial reasons to secure their future but also for his own benefit, as he was not a man to be idle. He was concerned that if he did eventually seek employment he would have to provide his correct name, and in his predicament that could in some way alert the police.

He wished to join the local Ambleside running club, but again if he used an alias that too could also eventually come back to haunt him.

With this in mind and looking to the future, he started to take note of the numerous minibus tours that operated around the lakes and local beauty spots. Dutch felt that driving, and informing tourists about such spectacular surroundings, and getting a financial reward for something so enjoyable, was not an opportunity he wanted to miss.

The thought of being a self-employed tour operator appealed to him, prompting him to make tentative enquiries regarding what process he would be required to follow for such a venture. Having noted a telephone number from a passing tour bus, he contacted the same Keswick based firm and spoke to the owner, Martin, who proved to be very friendly and helpful. He informed Dutch that to carry passengers he would need to obtain a public service vehicle driving licence, and an operator's licence. Dutch also asked advice regarding recommended vehicles for such work. Then Martin dropped a bombshell, by informing Dutch that, in addition to the licences mentioned, if he were to carry groups of children, the driver of such trips would require to be checked and accredited by the Disclosure and Barring Service.

A now concerned Dutch thanked Martin for his advice, realising that if he were to pursue this new career he would have to either submit to such a DBS check, which would alert the police to his present whereabouts, or somehow avoid carrying any parties of children, which would not only cause him to be viewed with suspicion, but could also place him in a very awkward position if refusing to do so. The only other alternative would be to give himself up to the police at a time and date of his choosing, in the hope that they had no evidence to link him to any of the fatalities.

The conversation troubled him as this was the first occasion since their move that he had to seriously consider the option that he had no idea of what the final result could be.

With such thoughts he located Melanie and informed her of the conversation and his heightened concerns.

"I really don't know what to do. As you know it was always my intention to settle us all in here and then go back and face the consequences, but we are all so happy and content and I don't feel I want to risk losing all that for what could possibly be a long term in jail."

Melanie grasped his hand and in gentle manner replied, "I don't know what to say. This is not a normal everyday dilemma for anyone to face. Of course, I don't want you to give yourself up, with the chance I may only see you inside of prison walls for years to come especially as, wrong as it was what you did, you did it to avenge what happened to me. But on the other hand, this is the first example of what can occur while you've got this problem hanging over your head, and I'm sure that there will be many more similar incidents to come. Can you live with that thought?"

"No, today is the day that I must make the decision I have been dreading for over two years. I don't want to do it as I'm so settled here, but knowing that you are all safe and happy gives me the strength to face the music. I am going to contact a solicitor in Brighton and make arrangements to go back and just see what happens."

Melanie, with tears in her eyes and tightening her grip on his hand said, "Oh! Dennis are you sure? Don't make any rash decisions that you may regret."

"No it's not rash, we all knew that this time would come. I will turn myself in as soon as I have contacted a solicitor for advice as to how to set it up."

Now, Dutch had decided that both his family were settled in their new surroundings and sufficient time had elapsed for nature and the weather to cover any signs of his presence near Lakeside Cottage, he telephoned the offices of Timothy Hunt Solicitors in Brighton. Following a lengthy conversation with Mr Hunt, Dutch was assured by the solicitor that he would enquire if in fact he was officially wanted by the police and if so he would make an appointment for Dutch to surrender himself at Brighton Police Station, at a time and date convenient for all parties.

Following this conversation, Dutch prepared a rucksack with all the essentials that he would require for his possible return to Sussex. He would be able to travel light, as he had left some clothing in the wardrobe in the spare bedroom at Jeanette's home in anticipation of such a return.

Chapter 14
Rescue Me (2011)

Artists: Daughtry
Writers: Christopher Daughtry, Josh Steely

DS Cannan was about to leave her office when she answered a call from the station officer at Brighton Police Station, who requested her to take a call from a solicitor named Timothy Hunt. The officer went on to explain that Hunt had asked him if any police officer wished to speak to a client of his named Dennis French. He had checked the name and date of birth given by Hunt against the data contained on the police national computer, which revealed that French was wanted by her for questioning regarding five deaths two years previously. She listened to him in almost disbelief, and somewhat quizzically asked for the solicitor to be put through. The conversation between Hunt and herself was brief and formal, with neither party discussing very much else other than arranging the venue and a mutual time and date for the officer to interview French the following week.

The call had puzzled Cannan as to how soon French had suddenly emerged, only having recently mentioned him as possibly being connected to the deaths of Stanescu and Gheata. Now it appeared that he had returned to the UK. and was surrendering himself for questioning regarding the murders of five other men, who were in various ways connected to the rape of his wife some two years earlier. She immediately passed this information to DCI Byrne and DI Woodall, who met her the following day in company with DC Buttle, to discuss the decisive points to be covered during the impending interview. During the conversation, the soon to be retired DCI mentioned that he could not obviously condone the killings of those who committed the rape of Melanie and their abetters, and the person or persons responsible should be brought to justice. However, owing to the brutality and the callousness involved he did have some empathy, if in fact it was her husband responsible for their deaths.

Woodall then took the opportunity to mention that PS Ramiz had made good progress with the coroners enquiry, as both deceased had been formally identified, a post-mortem had been completed and relatives of both men had been traced and informed of the circumstances of their demise.

On receiving a call from Tim Hunt, Dutch was given the news that he was officially wanted by the police and arrangements were made for him to meet at the solicitor's office the following week to prepare their case before meeting the investigating officers the following day. It was the news that he and Melanie had been dreading, but both knew that it was a step that had to be taken to release them from the uncertainty that would otherwise haunt them forever more.

Dutch decided that due to the possible consequences of his chosen option: if he remained in Cumbria any longer he or Melanie may be tempted to renege on their decision. To prevent prolonging his moment of departure, he promptly purchased an advanced rail ticket to Brighton and when doing so was astonished at the high cost of the fare, as he had not completed any long-distance train travel since his army days when he had then considered such fares reasonable. Melanie had suggested that he took her car but he declined the invitation, as if he were to be remanded in custody she would have to travel the long distance herself to collect it. For the same reason he purchased a single train ticket only, because if the police had sufficient evidence to remand him in custody, and if he was eventually convicted of the murders, a return ticket would never be of use to him.

On the morning of his departure, Dutch awoke early and after saying his agonising farewells to his in-laws and Jodie,

Melanie drove him along the northern shores of Lake Windermere to Burneside Station where, due to her considerable upset, he could have easily changed his mind, but after a heartfelt embrace together with her blessing, he reluctantly boarded the train.

During the long, uneventful four-and-a-half-hour journey to the south coast, he felt for his service identification tag that still hung around his neck and as he pinched the round metal disc, he thought of the Latin words 'Utrinque Paratus' which is the motto of the Para troop regiment meaning 'Ready for Anything', at the same time wondering if he really was prepared for the worst case scenario. On his arrival in Brighton, Dutch's sister Jeanette gave him a warm and sincere welcome back into her home, to which she had agreed via a telephone call from Mr Hunt that if necessary, Dutch could provide her address to the police as his place of residence. All parties concerned were aware that a bona fide place of residence was imperative if he were to be considered for bail, should certain conditions and restrictions be imposed. With a few days to spare before his meeting with his solicitor, he took the opportunity to attempt to regain some of his lost fitness by running on his beloved South Downs, the local beach and even a session on the local Withdean athletic stadium track on which International runners such as Chris Carter, Peter Standing, Steve Overt and so many other good athletes had trained and raced in the past. Apart from his running, Dutch kept a low profile within the city, as the last thing he required was to get picked up before speaking at length to his brief, as he considered that he would appear in a better light if he were to voluntarily surrender himself for the interview rather than being arrested on the street and giving the appearance of a desperate fugitive.

With this in mind, and time on his hands, Dutch invited Roy to join him in a visit to the nearby sedate seaside resort of Worthing, where he felt he could remain anonymous. Nonetheless, as a precaution he wore a baseball cap and sunglasses. It had been a perfect day in the company of his brother, even though Roy was regarded as a wayward character, he had remained a joy for Dutch to be with; and for the first time in a long time he felt a brotherly affection towards him, just as he had when they were youngsters. Following a pub lunch and exploring the shops, they headed for the town's 300-metre-length pier to play the slot machines.

The brothers were busy playing the low-level stake entertainment games when they became aware of loud shouting from outside of the amusement hall. On seeing people leaving through the door in the direction from where the commotion was coming, both Roy and Dutch, feeling inquisitive, also ventured out of the building onto the wooden plank walkway where a small crowd were looking over the guard rail out to sea.

On reaching the rail, Dutch immediately spotted a young boy alone in a small orange inflatable dingy in excess of half way along the length of the pier. He also noticed that the weather had become overcast and the wind speed had increased dramatically since he entered the building, causing a large swell which was moving the dinghy and the boy further out to sea and towards the side of the pier.

Dutch could see and hear from his shouts that the boy was extremely upset and gripping on tightly to a cord that was threaded around the circumference of the craft. Dutch became very concerned that the small boat was in imminent danger of toppling over in the ever increasing high white-capped waves, or may get pushed into the metal pier supports at such a speed that it would both throw the youngster out and puncture his only support in what was fast becoming difficult waters to stay afloat in for very long without a buoyancy aid.

After confirming with the throng of onlookers, who were shouting encouragement to the boy, that the emergency services had been informed, and thinking that the professional help may not arrive in time, Dutch kicked off his shoes, removed his sun glasses, hat and sweater, then handed the items together with the contents of his trouser pockets to his brother. Roy did not try to dissuade his brother from what he knew he was about to do, as he knew the look of determination on his face and was well aware that once Dutch had made up his mind, nobody was going to change his intentions. After passing his belongings to Roy, Dutch instructed him to find a red and white lifebuoy which should be prominently positioned somewhere on the pier, and if possible, depending on the strength and direction of the wind, to throw it into the water as close as he could to him. Dutch then, to the astonishment of the gathering, climbed the guard rail, lowered himself down then turned his body to face the sea. As he did so, he held on to the rail with both arms stretched behind him with his heels on the edges of the boards. He momentarily looked towards the beach and saw what he presumed was a frantic mother with others, waist deep in the water which was at high tide, screaming loudly in the direction of the stranded lad. At the same time he noted that there were no immediate signs of assistance coming from the beach or elsewhere.

Although he had attended courses in self survival techniques, in the cold seas of the Welsh coast, it was a long time since he swam in dangerous waters but was confident in his own ability to stay afloat, and certainly could not contemplate seeing the boy fall overboard and possibly drown without attempting to avoid a tragedy. His major concern was to be able to propel himself out and away from the pier as far as was possible, as he did not want to be immediately forced back into the rusty structure by the wind and waves before he had even attempted the rescue.

It was with some trepidation when Dutch released his grip on the rail and at the same time by bending his legs, pushed himself as hard as he possibly could away from the boards. As an ex-paratrooper the height of the drop was of no concern to him, in fact, he wished he could have been higher so he could have had more time to position his body to make a comfortable entry into the water.

During that brief moment in mid-air, he not only prepared himself for the impact on hitting the water but also braced himself for what he knew was going to be a shock to his warm body on entry into the ice-cold sea.

Dutch hit the water, feet first in a vertical position, and due to the height of his jump sunk deeper than he had anticipated. Having forced himself to the surface, the sudden submersion and extreme cold caused him to take a few seconds to catch his breath. Then having normalised his breathing and gained his bearings, he caught sight of the dinghy, now even further out from the shore, being perilously tossed up and down on the sizeable waves.

The boy had obviously seen him jump from the pier as he was looking and shouting inaudibly in his direction. Dutch took some deep breaths and then started to front crawl swim away from the nearby pier towards his target. He found it an effort to swim against both the strong crosswind and the undercurrent and was only making slow headway, and as he progressed Dutch would every now and again shout words of reassurance to the youngster, who now seeing Dutch approaching appeared calmer. The sea conditions were so tough that every now and again Dutch would have to stop swimming to take some deep breaths before resuming his pursuit of the dinghy. On some occasions his pursuit was hampered when the wind caught the dinghy broadside and blew it further away from the would-be rescuer.

When he eventually reached the dinghy, Dutch was breathing heavily and feeling extremely cold, but to see and hear the relief that the youngster was expressing made him forget any of his own discomfort. Dutch was pleased to be able to gain a little support from the inflatable himself, which made him realise how his fitness levels had dropped since leaving the army. Dutch established that the boy's name was Paul and was on a day trip from London with his mother, who had purchased the dinghy for him only hours before. Paul had launched it from the beach, and before he knew it he was being swept out into deep waters, and being only a weak swimmer had sensibly remained in the small boat.

During the little time that he spent talking to the boy and treading water, they were continually being pushed towards the pier and their progress was being followed by onlookers high above them. On looking up Dutch saw Roy holding the lifebuoy that he had described to him. The brothers were both shouting at each other, but the noise of the crashing waves against the pier supports and the din created by the numerous now interested seagulls made it impossible to hear what each was saying. As conversation proved impossible, Dutch, by raising his arm, indicated for Roy to throw him the buoyancy aid. Understanding the gesture, Roy waited for a momentary drop in the wind and tossed the buoy out as far as he was able towards them.

By more luck than judgement it proved to be an expert throw and did not take an excessive effort for Dutch to tow the dinghy and retrieve the buoy, which he passed to the young lad and instructed him how to wear it. Having walked around the pier before entering the amusement arcade, Dutch knew that at the end of the pier there was a lower level platform constructed of thick wooden supports for mooring small boats and for the use of rod and line fishermen. Dutch realised that reaching the platform was going to his best option, rather than trying to attempt the long and difficult swim back to the shore. With this in mind he raised his arm from the water and by pointing indicated to Roy to make his way there. Dutch then kept himself and the dinghy as close to the pier as he could without being swept into it. As they drifted closer to the end of the pier, the fishermen's level came into view, where he could see his brother at the front of the waiting crowd.

As the wind was continually pushing the dinghy further out into deeper water, it was now time for Dutch to dispense with the craft in order for him to have more control over reaching his desired destination. Dutch made sure that the buoy was tucked tightly under the youngster's arms, then instructed him how to slide over the side of the boat into the sea. As a junior soldier he had gained the gold medallion award for life-saving training skills and could still remember how to hold and tow a person in difficulty without a bouncy aid, but the success of such techniques depended very much on if the stranded person panicked or not. All such training had been completed in indoor and outdoor pools, not in such conditions as he was now experiencing. Dutch, who now had a firm hold of the long cord attached to the buoy, encouraged the reluctant shivering and soaking wet youngster into the water. Dutch was now close enough to the lower level to let go of the water-filled and ever-deflating craft, which once acted as an aide, but now in their present situation was becoming a hindrance. Dutch could now see some long rusty metal steps attached to a thick wooden foundation post which led down into the water, but the swell around the area was extreme, and as he felt himself weakening he knew how extremely difficult it would be for him to get the frightened boy and himself onto the ladder through such conditions without being tossed into the thick wooden supports.

As Dutch looked towards Roy, who was already half way down the ladder, encouraging him by way of waving an outstretched arm, he saw a young man on the fishing platform stripping off to his underpants, something he wished he had done himself, as his sodden jeans had been a burden throughout. He then saw the man expertly dive into the water and immediately swim towards them at speed. Dutch was delighted to see such an able swimmer approaching them, realising that he now had the assistance they required to reach the steps. On sensing that Dutch was exhausted, the new rescuer took control of the buoy and the youngster within, and with fresh arms and legs pushed them through the swell to the steps where Roy was waiting to assist the lad to the top into the arms of his waiting fretful and tearful mother. Dutch, who was now tired and struggling in the wash created by the returning waves as they crashed into the wooden staging, made one final effort and swam towards the ladder, where he was grateful to be met by the swimmer who assisted him in grabbing onto one of the ladder rungs.

After a very brief chat, Dutch was the first of the two men to emerge from the water. He climbed the ladder onto the decking, where he was immediately greeted by a spontaneous applause from the large crowd that had congregated. Feeling both embarrassed and exhausted, he sat with Roy discussing both the incident and how uncomfortable he was going to be travelling home that evening in soaking wet trousers. During their chat and dressing in the dry items that Roy had retained for him, Dutch was approached by Paul and his mother who both expressed their upmost gratitude to him. During the conversation Dutch jokingly apologised for failing to rescue the newly purchased dinghy, but on the other hand due to what had occurred mentioned that perhaps it was a good thing that it was no longer available to Paul. Before leaving him, and despite his wet condition, Paul's mother gave Dutch a prolonged hug, and noticing that he had no towel on which to dry himself took one from a large bag, which she handed to him and insisted he kept. A grateful Dutch started to dry himself, and the brothers were just planning their exit when they were approached by a young woman, who identified herself as being a freelance reporter from the local newspaper. Stating that she wished to write an article on the rescue, she began to ask Dutch for some of his details. Immediately seeing the danger of his name and photograph being seen by either the police or any of the remaining Romanian gang, he suggested that she should interview the mother and her son, and also the other rescuer who remained nearby, while he continued to dry himself, then after doing so he would return to her. Satisfied with his proposal, the reporter made herself known to the other parties.

As Dutch and Roy began a surreptitious exit away from the gathering, they saw the approaching inshore lifeboat and could also hear the distant sound of a helicopter. Not wishing to be subject to any more attention, the brothers hurried off the pier into the town centre and into the nearest department store. After informing Roy of his trouser size, Dutch located the changing room where he removed his sodden jeans and underpants and continued to dry himself with the gifted towel. Having purchased the garment they both returned to Brighton, after a far more exciting day than they had anticipated.

Dutch had quietly enjoyed the praise bestowed on him, just as he had done when awarded his past military honour, but this particular accolade would have to remain a relative secret because of the precarious predicament that he had created for himself. When he spoke of the incident with Melanie, during the conversation she said, "It's unfortunate that you were forced to shun the publicity, as it would have given an indication to the imminent investigation as to the true caring side of your character, and not that of a cold blooded killer that they will believe you to be."

Dutch after some thought, "You know, Melanie, you having said that, has made me think that not only did I rescue Paul out in that sea today, but perhaps in some way it has rescued me as well, by knowing that perhaps I saved a life rather than taking one."

Chapter 15
Under Pressure (1981)

Artists: Queen and David Bowie
Writers: Roger Taylor, Freddie Mercury

Dutch's eventual meeting with Tim Hunt started as a formal affair, but after the solicitor obtained all the required essential information the consultation became much friendlier and less business-like, creating a relaxed ambience. As Dutch had mentioned his recent employment in Venezuela, the discussion turned to the political turmoil in the country, where there was even a food shortage for much of the population. The mention of the crisis made Dutch consider if Holton, George and 'Bo' would, as a result, experience increasing attacks from what would be even more desperate criminal gangs. Among other topics they spoke about were the exploits of the local football club, Brighton and Hove Albion. Hunt also made the connection between Dutch and his brother Roy, who he had represented several times in the past. Dutch left the meeting as confident as he could be, considering he had no idea as to what evidence the police had to offer the following day.

At 10:00 a.m. the solicitor and his client met outside of the police station in John Street, with Dutch immediately confirming that he had remembered to bring his passport. Once inside of the busy public waiting area, they spoke to the female civilian member of staff on duty at the front desk who was expecting them and immediately made an internal telephone call. Within minutes of the call the stocky, bearded and smart-suited figure of DC Roger Buttle emerged from an internal door marked 'custody suite' and ushered both men inside. Having closed the door to prevent the proceedings being witnessed by other members of the public, the introductions took place. This was followed by the detective saying to Dutch, "Dennis French, I am arresting you on suspicion of the murders of..." Then, after referring to a sheet of paper, read out five foreign sounding names that included the name Ivan Stanescu. He then cautioned French who made no reply.

All three then approached the custody desk, where the custody sergeant informed French of his rights, which was followed by DC Buttle searching him and handing over the small amount of property found on his person to the sergeant, which included French's passport. During this search, Buttle took the opportunity to note the size of the shoe that French was wearing. Following an exchange of signatures and official papers, the trio entered a nearby interview room in which DS Cannan, who had in the past briefly spoken to French following the rape of his wife sat waiting.

Once all were seated, following formal introductions Cannan explained that the interview was to be recorded both visually and audibly, French was again reminded of why he had been arrested and further cautioned.

In reply Hunt said to the officers, "My client, Mr French, has prepared a short statement which is as follows." The solicitor then read from the piece of notepaper. "I do not wish to appear rude or disrespectful, but at this stage I will not be answering any questions put to me today." Hunt then handed the paper signed by French to the officers.

Cannan, referring her remarks to French, replied, "That is your prerogative under law, but we must still ask you all of what we consider are relevant questions regarding the offences that you have been arrested for."

The interview commenced with both officers outlining the circumstances of the case, asking French numerous questions concerning his whereabouts on both dates and times when the five fatalities occurred.

He was further asked if he could provide any alibis as to his location at the relevant times. French answered all with the same reply of *No comment.*

When Buttle read out the names of the five deceased and enquired if French had any knowledge of any of them, he again responded in an identical manner.

Now, knowing that one of the men who died in the burning cabin was named Ivan Stanescu, Dutch realised that this was the name given to the Stan that had been mentioned by one of the two that he shot when they were about to rape a woman in the back of a van on Devil's Dyke. He also recalled a silver Porsche with the distinctive personalised registration number of B00 5TAN that he had seen on three occasions at the car wash site on the Riverside Industrial Estate in Lewes, which he had correctly considered had appertained to the same man.

During the lengthy interview, Dutch sensed the frustration of the interviewing officers at his monotonous and monotone answers. He himself did not like answering every question in this manner and had never liked watching accused persons in TV dramas or documentaries answering in the same way, but with the stakes so high he could not afford to drop his guard and make a careless comment that could incriminate himself, as he had no idea what, if any evidence, the police were in possession of.

Buttle asked his shoe size and after receiving an identical response to the question, then added that during the earlier search he was aware that Dutch was wearing size nine shoes.

It was at this stage when the interviewing officers mentioned the rape and serious assault that had been inflicted on Melanie, suggesting that Dutch had managed to trace the two perpetrators, shooting those dead when they attempted to carry out an identical attack on a further woman. They added that the offender left a size nine shoe print in the mud at the scene, the same size as the shoes that he was wearing.

Met again with an identical response, they continued to speak about the three men who had been locked in a porta cabin at a car wash site situated at Riverside Industrial Estate in Lewes, where the cabin was deliberately set alight and the three had perished in the fire. They went on to add that all five deceased worked for the same company, and the three in the porta cabin were believed to be involved in the handling and distribution of film showing the rape of his wife.

It saddened French to listen to these facts. He so wished he could have told the officers, yes, I did it and I have no regrets in doing so. Would you not have wished to have had such revenge if similar had happened to a loved one? It was my only option for any kind of retribution, as Melanie was in no mental or physical state to be a witness at court. However, he fully understood that both officers had a job to do and would possibly fully agree with his actions had they been in a different occupation.

French was then asked if he had ever visited the Riverside Industrial Area. Having again received a no comment reply, Buttle produced from a box file an invoice contained in a clear plastic bag with an exhibit label attached. As soon as French saw the item he recognised that it was the invoice for a part to a water pump that he had purchased for his boss at the time, Jon Shipway. French was aware that it had been discovered amongst paperwork when the police searched Jon's office. Shortly after buying and signing for the part he had noticed the car wash, and as he suspected that his wife's assailants worked in such an occupation he visited the site and it was then he identified his wife's description of the men and vehicle involved.

French was asked if he agreed that he had purchased and signed for the product on that day, only to receive another no comment reply. The detective then stated that the invoice containing his signature showed that he was on the same industrial estate on a Friday, exactly three weeks following his wife's ordeal, where the two men known to have been responsible for the rape worked. Buttle put it to him that he went to the car wash where they were employed and somehow recognised the men responsible, and that a week later he shot them in a van while they were engaged in the attack on another woman.

French was aware from Jon that the police were in possession of the invoice, which not only bore his signature but when forensically examined would no doubt reveal his fingerprints. To hear the fact mentioned in such a manner, coupled with the known shoe size, was now sounding quite damning, and he thought that he sensed an anxiousness in his solicitor's movements, but he considered that it was probably his own concerns making himself feel uneasy.

French was then asked about his previous army career and if he had possessed a firearm since leaving the army. All questions were again answered in the same manner.

The interrogation then centred on his previous works van and how similar it was to one captured on CCTV driving away from the burning porta cabin in which the three men died and displaying false number plates. The officers stated that the plates had been obtained from a Pease Pottage vehicle salvage yard and they were aware from invoices removed from his ex-employer's office that the company regularly purchased items from the yard. It was put to French that he had visited the scrap yard and removed plates from an identical van to his work vehicle and swapped them for the purpose of travelling to and from the scene of the fire for which he was responsible. Mention was also made of his seemingly hasty departure to Venezuela only hours after the fire, a country that had no extradition agreement with the UK.

French again did not respond, but he now realised that the police had pieced together much of what he had done but as yet did not appear to have enough evidence to charge or convict him. He hoped that his past study in forensic science, when once considering leaving the army to join the police service, had assisted him in avoiding leaving any such clues. His thoughts were that if they had discovered any fingerprints or forensic evidence that connected him to either scene, surely they would have revealed as much by now, or were they playing a waiting game and about to release their ace cards?

Then came the bombshell. Having closed one of the files on the desk in front of him, Buttle then opened another, and following a brief examination of them the officer then said, "I am now arresting you on suspicion of being concerned in the murder of Yannis Stanescu and Alexe Gheata at Lakeside Cottage, Albourne." He again cautioned French, who attempted to hide his utter surprise as to how they had connected him to the deaths, and also to the fact that the name Stanescu had been mentioned once again. French quickly gathered his thoughts, looked towards his solicitor and said, "No reply."

It was at this point that his solicitor Mr Hunt intervened and asked that as the interview had already been lengthy, and due to this notification of a further arrest, he suggested that his client be allowed a temporary break from the proceedings. During the interval Hunt suggested that French continued to respond to the questions in the same way as before, and as the interview progressed they would be able to establish why they suspected that he may be involved. During this conversation French's thoughts were in turmoil, constantly searching his mind for a reason as to how they had made the connection. Was it somehow involving the name Stanescu?

When both officers returned to the room the recordings were again activated, and after Dutch was reminded of what he had further been arrested for and cautioned, the proceedings resumed.

DS Cannan, who was now in possession of French's passport said after closely examining the pages of the document, "We have checked with the immigration authorities and there is no record of where or when you re-entered the UK. Can you explain this?"

Again French answered, "No comment."

Amongst the numerous questions that both officers asked were had French any knowledge of Albourne and the Ferguson brothers, and had he ever telephoned them? Where was he at particular times and dates, and did he have alibis to confirm his whereabouts at the times given? One question that surprised him, and made him realise that the investigating officers had been very thorough in their work, was when he was asked if he had recently had access to or driven a white motor home? He had seen the motor home leave the scene almost immediately following the shootings but could not yet understand how they had obtained the information. Had they apprehended the Watchman, had the Fergusons done what he thought unlikely and bubbled him up? He had been sure that the Fergusons would not have ratted on the Watchman because, as tough as they both thought they were, surely even they would have been reluctant to attempt to implicate such an expert practitioner of his trade, considering the possible repercussions?

Once again the continual flow of questions received the identical and monotonous statement of no reply.

The DS then asked if he knew either Ivan or Yannis Stanescu, to which she received the identical reply that had been repeated throughout the entire interview. She went on to explain that Yannis was one of the two men shot and killed at Albourne and was the younger brother of Ivan, who was known to be in possession of a film of the rape of his wife and died in the arson attack at the industrial estate.

This revelation answered a question that was to renew his confidence, that perhaps he was not being pursued by the foreign gang that he had attacked and exposed to the British authorities; but there had been more of a personal reason behind the threat. Such pleasing thoughts that the threat to him and his family had now diminished were soon to be shattered. Then came the exposure of the one flaw in his well-executed plan. He always knew that it was a risk, but he had no other way of carrying out the hoax.

When questioned regarding his access to his in-laws' bungalow at Cowley Drive, he again failed to give an answer. This was followed by the officers stating that they were aware that it was the address at which his wife stayed with her parents shortly after she was raped, up until her departure to join him in Venezuela. French was then asked if he knew a Donald McKinnon, to which he responded in an identical manner. This proved to be another shock to French, who attempted to hide the fact by acting nonchalant, but at the same time presuming that as the name McKinnon and Cowley Drive had been mentioned in quick succession, that this must be the man he had nicknamed Nesbitt, but how had they made the connection between them both?

He was soon to discover how, when he was informed that it was McKinnon who lived in the bungalow almost opposite his in-laws' address, and two days before the double fatality at Lakeside Cottage had taken place, a telephone call was made from McKinnon's address to a mobile telephone. Enquiries had revealed that the call had been made to a mobile owned by Yannis Stanescu, who was one of the two men shot dead. French was asked if he could think of any reason as to why someone from a property so close to the vicinity of an address that he was connected to would call Yannis Stanescu, the brother of Ivan, who could be linked to the horrendous attack on his wife?

French again replied, "No comment." This gave French grave news about his future. What had been his greatest concern was now under the spotlight. If, despite his attempted disguise, McKinnon could identify him and could also remember the address that he had supposedly passed to a taxi company, would that coupled with other circumstantial evidence be enough to lead to a conviction?

The final question put to him was had he murdered any of the seven men, or had any involvement in their deaths?.

Dutch was prepared for this particular question, knowing this could be the opportunity to fervently deny the allegations put to him, but he would continue to play the waiting game. It may eventually come to a point where the evidence against him was so overwhelming that he may need to come clean and admit all in an attempt to reduce the term of a prison sentence.

Again the question received a no-comment response.

At the conclusion of the interview, after the recordings had been switched off, French and his solicitor were informed by the officers that it would be necessary for them to seek advice regarding future proceedings. They suggested that during these discussions, they would arrange for French's fingerprints and photograph to be taken, and following deliberation between client and solicitor a decision would have been made. After completing the identification procedures, French was returned to the interview room where he and Hunt entered into a discussion regarding the interview. Hunt reminded him that all his links to the offences found by the police so far were purely circumstantial. Both were confused as to why the name and address of Donald McKinnon had been mentioned, but no further questions were asked, and his possible involvement in the case was not touched on again. Although, French of course could not reveal his guilt to his solicitor, and what damning evidence McKinnon could provide to the police. He was, however, able to inform Hunt that he was aware that McKinnon had been evicted from the Cowley Drive address. Both men agreed that perhaps the reason that McKinnon had not continued to feature in the interview was because his present whereabouts was unknown to the police.

After Cannan and Buttle had reported the content of the interview to Woodall, he then in turn relayed the facts to the Crown Prosecution Service solicitor. Following this discussion, the interviewing officers were made aware of the decision as to future proceedings and both returned to the cell block.

In the presence of Hunt, French was informed that it had been decided to grant him bail with the following conditions, whilst their enquiries into the matters continued: To return to Brighton Police Station in four weeks, to reside at his sister's home in Chapel Street, to surrender his passport, report to Brighton Police Station each Wednesday and Saturday and not to make contact, or attempt to make contact, with any prosecution witnesses, including Mr Donald McKinnon.

French was delighted to have been granted bail, which was a good start to his efforts to escape conviction for the crimes that he had felt forced to commit for revenge, and latterly for the protection of his wife and her parents. As pleased as he was at the decision, the downside was the condition that reporting to the police station twice during each week for a month would mean that he would have to restrict his visits to Cumbria, as there would be little time to spend with his family, and hardly worth the two days' travel and expense for such a short visit.

Once he had confirmed and signed the bail notice accepting the conditions imposed, he handed his passport to the police officers. French signed the necessary custody record, then having received his retained property, Hunt and himself then left the building.

Before parting, they spoke about the bail condition preventing French from contacting McKinnon, and discussed if this meant that the police did possibly know of his whereabouts, or were they hoping to locate him within the four weeks? Neither man could think as to what other enquiries were required that could possibly take the police such a time to complete.

Having made future arrangements, both men shook hands and parted, prompting Dutch to immediately telephone his worried and patiently waiting wife. Melanie was ecstatic at the outcome and was immediately able to put his mind at rest regarding his problem about him returning, as both she and her parents had a few outstanding matters they needed to personally attend to in Sussex, so they would travel down themselves in two weeks and see him during their temporary stay.

Chapter 16
Red Wine (1983)

Artists: UB40
Writers: Neil Diamond

Dutch had a feeling of great relief, but after what had been over two years of concern regarding the outcome of his first meeting with police, he knew he was far from being out of the woods yet. He realised that apart from the possible devastating result that the tracing of McKinnon may reveal, there was still one slight concern that could connect him to the Fergusons and the scene of the double killing. Shortly after the Fergusons had moved into Lakeside Cottage, and because of their intention to turn it into a fishery, Dutch had worked there on the drainage and water supply for the lake for the company owned by his friend, Jon Shipway. It had always been in the back of his mind that the police might discover this fact, which would obviously connect him to both the location and the brothers, who he had met while working there. He had always hoped that there was no further paper work in existence to show either his or the company's involvement in this work, as he knew that when Jon had approached them for payment, Daniel Ferguson had ripped up his copy of the invoice and at the same time threatened Jon with violence. The fact that this had not yet been mentioned reassured his thoughts on the matter.

DCs Reay and Bye were sat side-by-side scrutinising computer data, in an attempt to trace a similar modus operandi to that of a series of aggravated burglaries that they were investigating, when they were approached by their DI.

After the officers had informed him of their present task, Woodall said to both, "I know that you both like to do your own background work, but on this occasion I would like you to leave this part of your investigation in the hands of the crime analyst, as I have a very pressing job that needs to be done. Is there any reason why either of you two reprobates can't go on a road trip for a few days?"

Reay, having received a nod of agreement from his partner replied, "Plods on tour, sounds good to us, guv."

"It's nothing too glamorous I'm afraid. I need you both to get up to Scotland in relation to the Ferguson case and trace this McKinnon fella that you are both aware of."

Bye replied, "I only agreed to go as I thought it may be to the Caribbean or somewhere like that, but Scotland is good."

"Gary, if it had been somewhere exotic I would have wangled doing the enquiry myself. Anyway, back to business. We flagged McKinnon's name to the Scottish forces, and after making enquiries with their work and pensions departments, they have recently received information from them that McKinnon has an appointment at the Inverness office in two days' time. This gives you both enough time to familiarise yourself with the case, especially the part that he may play in it, get packed and get your arses up there in one of the pool cars. Also, you best go and see the collator immediately, and get him to locate the recent custody photo taken of Dennis French and ask him to make up and include it in a photo ID album for you to take. We need to know if McKinnon knows French, or ever came in contact with him around the time of the offences. If so, exactly what was said? Are you both still here?"

The officers quickly closed down their computer, collected their paperwork and were about to leave their desk when Woodall said, "And I don't want your expenses for this trip reflecting in the taking of any Scottish falling down water."

Bye immediately quipped, "You know us, guv, Irn Bru only."

Woodall chuckled as they both left the room.

*****

In the meantime, Dutch was not one to be idle, and as much as he enjoyed Brighton he didn't relish the thought of having so much time on his hands. With this in mind he spoke to Jeanette and Roy and arranged that at his expense, he would fulfil his promise of taking them both to visit their half brother and sister in Wiltshire. Having contacted Deborah and Barry, he was able to confirm with all that as soon as he had fulfilled his bail commitment on Wednesday morning, Jeanette would drive them to a hotel in Swindon where he had reserved a single and a double room for two nights.

Swindon, an interesting town with a famous rail museum set in a restored station, was somewhere Dutch had always wished to visit and explore, as was the nearby market town of Royal Wootton Bassett, which appealed to his military interest. The latter had been granted royal patronage in 2011, in recognition of its role in the military funeral repatriations of service men killed in Afghanistan which passed through the town. It was somewhere that Dutch had always wanted to visit to pay tribute. Perhaps, by luck, and despite many attempts by opposing forces, he would unlike so many of his colleagues from the war in Afghanistan, be able to walk the High Street known as the 'Highway of Heroes'.

As Deborah and Barry now lived close to each other in the village of Blunsdon, situated only four miles from Swindon town centre, the hotel proved to be an ideal location for their planned reunion. The two groups of siblings, who were tragically separated when very young, had not met for many years, and it proved to be a very emotional occasion as they discussed both their parents' tragic deaths and how grateful they all were for their relatives stepping in and securing their futures. They all agreed that their grandparents Connie and Sinbad held a special place in their hearts. Both Deborah and Barry now had families of their own, who made them all very welcome when visiting their respective homes. Dutch found it interesting that Deborah, the eldest of the five, and as young as she was at the time of their troubled past, had always been an authoritative and caring person to them all, and despite all the years that had passed she was still held in the same high regard by her siblings.

Before they departed from Wiltshire, which they all agreed had been a wonderful and fulfilling occasion, Dutch paid a visit to Wootton Bassett and solemnly laid a memorial wreath in the nearby field of remembrance.

During the period of his police bail, Dutch, together with Jon, was able to carry out long-awaited visits to two former colleagues with whom they had both served in Iraq and Afghanistan. David Crook, who was nicknamed Davy Crockett, had been medically discharged from the army after being diagnosed as suffering from Post-Traumatic Stress Disorder, caused when caught in an ambush by Islamic State insurgents. Three of his unit were killed and his colleague James Bird, nicknamed Dickie, had lost a leg. It had been necessary for Jon and Dutch to contact the Forces Defence Medical Rehabilitation Centre at RAF Headley Court to establish their present whereabouts, but due to the time lapse it proved difficult to locate them. Both friends were eventually traced, and despite both casualties of war putting on a brave face in the presence of their visitors, both Jon and Dutch were disappointed in the lack of after care and financial help that both worthy parties were receiving from any of the governmental departments, with both men heavily relying on armed forces charities for assistance. The circumstances left both of the visitors saddened after what was otherwise a joyous reunion.

*****

On their return from Scotland, Bye and Reay approached Woodall in his office and handed him the written statement dictated and signed by Donald McKinnon. In their presence, the inspector scrutinised the document with great interest.

After the preamble which included McKinnon's full name, age and address, the statement went on to explain how between eighteen months to a year before, as he was leaving his home in Cowley Drive, he was approached by two men who he described as having what he considered were Bulgarian or Romanian accents. The men had pointed out the bungalow situated opposite his and explained that the daughter of the occupants was married to a man who owed a great deal of money, and the two men had been hired by an insurance company to trace him in order to collect the debt. They offered him £250 to report any sightings of the husband, and if he did so, and they were successful in tracing him, he would receive a further identical amount for his troubles. McKinnon stated that as he had been unemployed for a considerable time, he was grateful for the offer and took the initial cash payment. He added that as soon as he had received the money, both men took on a more intimidating persona, indicating that having received the money if he failed to comply there would be physical repercussions. He was handed a small card on which only a telephone number was printed. He had kept the card in his wallet in case he should see the man they desired to trace, but he had since destroyed the card. He went on to describe the spokesman of the two, which fitted Stanescu, and the other person described resembled Gheata. During this conversation, he was able to identify to the pair a woman who he presumed, as she returned to her parents' bungalow walking a dog, was the wife of the man that they wished to trace.

Due to his many personal problems, McKinnon had almost forgotten about the brief meeting when shortly before his eviction he saw a man leaving the bungalow concerned who asked him if he knew of a local taxi company. By his own admission, he was drunk at the time but was able to describe him as a little under six feet tall, mid-forties, medium build, medium-length light brown hair with a full beard, wearing a hat and glasses. He was unable to remember the exact conversation but could recall that the person had just fallen out with the occupants of the address that he had just left and required the number of a taxi company to take him to temporary rented accommodation. He provided the enquirer with the telephone number of Falcon Taxi Services, a company that he regularly used himself, and had overheard the address where he wished to be taken.

Believing this was the man Stanescu and Gheata sought, immediately following the conversation he had made a hurried phone call before he forgot the details of the intended destination. The male receiving the call did not identify himself but showed extreme interest in what he told him, and whatever little the receiver did say in return was in an identical accent to the men that had called upon him. He could not now remember any part of the address that he had overheard the person of interest requesting to be taken to, only that it had left him with the impression that it was in a rural location. Due to his impending eviction, it had occurred to him not to bother to report his sighting, but he was concerned that if he failed to do so, the two of whom he was fearful may, due to their apparent occupation, have the means to trace him. During his phone call he had not mentioned his imminent move, as he had no desire for them or others to know of his future whereabouts, even though it could mean him forfeiting any further payment.

Both DC s informed Woodall that when they interviewed McKinnon, despite his official attendance at the work and pensions office, he was clearly under the influence of alcohol and was in extremely poor health. He was at present living in a temporary hostel, and it came as no surprise to either of the officers when he informed them he was suffering from sclerosis of the liver due to alcohol abuse.

McKinnon was shown an album of twelve assorted photographs, one of which was the recent photograph taken of Dennis French whilst in police custody. As the image of French was clean-shaven with short hair and without glasses, all the accompanying photographs were of a similar appearance. McKinnon was unable to identify any of the images shown to him as being the person to whom he had spoken outside of his home in response to a request for information about a taxi service.

The officers also expressed their grave doubts of McKinnon being a credible witness. This was due not only to his obvious alcohol dependency and the failure to identify their suspect, but even if he was fortunate to live long enough to attend a trial he was now aware of the deaths and seriousness of the possible charges of all involved, and he stated that he would be very reluctant to attend any subsequent proceedings.

The interviewing officers mentioned that at one stage during the proceedings McKinnon had broken down in tears, blaming his addiction for the loss of his devoted wife and home and the comfortable lifestyle that he once enjoyed. Although, feeling for him, he on his own admission had made no attempt to seek help from the Alcoholics Anonymous organisation or anyone else and had no intentions of ever doing so.

To shed even further doubt on his credibility, the officers had carried out an enquiry with Falcon Taxis. According to McKinnon, he had dictated the telephone number of the company from their business card to the man they suspected was Dennis French. A subsequent enquiry found no such record of any of their taxis either going to Cowley Drive or to Albourne on the date that McKinnon had passed on his information to Stanescu's phone. Although, he had seen the person requesting the taxi enter a vehicle soon after their conversation, he could no longer remember the make, model or even colour of the vehicle. As a precaution the officers had carried out identical enquiries with the numerous taxi companies in the area, and none of their cabs had carried out that specific journey at the relevant time and date. Efforts were made to trace any CCTV footage between Cowley Drive and Albourne for the date in question but due to the time lapse such enquiries proved fruitless.

Both McKinnon himself and the contents of his statement proved to be a great disappointment to Woodall and his team, as they believed that coupled with the circumstantial evidence that had come to notice, if McKinnon had been a more sober and stable person he would have possibly remembered at least part of the address mentioned by the person he saw leaving a premises to which French could be connected. There still were a number of anomalies to the circumstances surrounding the meeting of McKinnon and the man that they believed to be French. Even if McKinnon was drunk at the time, how could he be so far out with his description of French? Or was he being evasive to avoid being called as a witness, or was French disguised in case the meeting should come to notice? These facts, together with the failure to find the supposed taxi, and the knowledge that Melanie and her family were in the Lake District at the time when McKinnon was adamant that the man he had described had emerged from the front door of their bungalow, after a supposed argument between him and the occupants, made no sense whatsoever.

The officers presumed that French would have some form of access to his in-laws' address, so had he devised a cunning plan to wipe out the threat of retribution from the Romanian gang, which happened to include the brother of one of his former victims? The police team discussed the many possible scenarios at length, but all agreed that there was no concrete evidence connecting either French to McKinnon or to any of the seven dead gang members. Having exhausted every possible line of enquiry the files were submitted to the Crown Prosecution Service solicitor, who after much deliberation reluctantly agreed that there was insufficient evidence to charge Dennis French with any of the offences of which he was suspected.

The recently retired ex-Chief Inspector Tony Byrne and his wife Christine had just returned from one of his bucket-listed visits to the Calgary Stampede when he received the call from Woodall, who had assured him that due to his initial involvement with the rape of Melanie French and the subsequent murders at Lakeside Cottage, he would keep him informed as to the final result of this momentous enquiry. On hearing that; although, the officers believed French had in some way been involved in all seven deaths, it had been decided that there would be no further action taken against him. Byrne had spent a life time fighting crime, but secretly on this occasion he was not sorry that French would never face justice. Although, he had never personally met French, he felt that from his team's intense enquiries about the man, he had formed the opinion that he was an ordinary, honest citizen; once of good character and an expert soldier who had fought for his country, but who was so consumed with hatred for the persons responsible for the horrific attack and for the demeaning film taken of his wife, that he had killed the men involved in the despicable act, and if not for his presence two of them would have done the same again to another innocent woman.

Byrne had also experienced the feeling of requiring revenge, although, on a much smaller scale; not against a criminal but a supposed colleague, when early in his police career he had been intensely investigated and accused of a crime he had not committed. From that day when the false accusation was made against him, because the matter had remained undetected, his anger had stayed within him; as he felt that any remaining suspicion from those who did not know him well would tarnish both his career and his impeccable character forever. He was indeed satisfied with the rank that he had attained but was sure that if not for the one slur on his character he could have received even further promotions. Although, the event occurred many years before, due to the manner in which he was treated by the leading investigating officer, his bitter feelings against that officer had never diminished and had remained so intense that he continued to wish great harm to befall him.

On the day that Dennis French answered his bail and was informed that no charges were to be made against him, he experienced a great sense of relief from a matter that had hung over him for more than two years. After receiving his passport and leaving the police station he was greeted by Melanie's open arms, who had without his knowledge travelled to Brighton, as she had wished to be present whatever the final outcome. After thanking his solicitor there were no celebrations, Dutch and his wife just walked into the city centre where they had a meal and were now able to freely discuss their future lives together without the fears that had formerly haunted them.

Chapter 17
Home (2003)

Artists: Simply Red
Writers: M Hucknall, S Lewinson, P Lewinson

Once they had returned to their new home, the couple were now able to be far more realistic but still cautious regarding their future. Knowing the reputation of the far-reaching tentacles of his determined pursuers, Dutch avoided every possible photograph, grew back his beard and longer hair, and abstained from giving out his address whenever possible. He even obtained a PO Box for some of his correspondence and opted out of the open electoral register. Although, in some cases relating to official documents such as his army pension he was required to give his correct address but felt such sensitive information would remain secure. He felt certain that he would have to maintain such precautions for years to come, but by and large he pushed the possible threat to the back of his mind.

Dutch, who was now in a position to pursue his new work venture, took his first step towards his new employment by taking and passing the Public Service Vehicle Driving Licence test, which was essential for him to carry fare-paying passengers. Having not been charged with any of the offences for which he had been arrested, he was able to apply and obtain a certificate from the Disclosure and Barring Service confirming that he had no criminal convictions that would prevent him from pursuing his chosen career. When initially making enquiries regarding the most suitable vehicle for such work, it had been recommended that he convert and customise a Mercedes

Sprinter to suit his own specifications. Following some research of this option and the viewing of similar vehicles, he contacted a local dealer and work commenced on his project.

During the wait for the conversion, Dutch telephone his good friend and ex-boss Jon Shipway to inform him of his new address and to offer an invite for both Jon and his wife Sally to visit them for a holiday at any time they wished. During the lengthy conversation Jon commented, "I'm pleased that you are finally settled. Considering what's happened to you in the past, both in the mob and after, you have been one very lucky fucker."

Dutch, after briefly hesitating, replied, "Mate that remark has just returned the favour similar to the one I did for you, when I came up with the idea for your company name. I now know what to call my new business."

"What lucky fucker? That will go down well with the punters. What sort of business are you going to be running there?"

"Sod off. I will let you know if it comes off, as I don't want you taking the piss if it all falls through."

Following further friendly banter the call concluded.

While patiently awaiting the completion of his newly adapted transport, Dutch continued his quest to regain some of the fitness that he considered he had lost over the years.

One early warm and misty morning, while searching for new training routes, Dutch was running across a paddock when, passing through a gap in a fallen stone wall, he saw a slim-built man who appeared to be in his early sixties, dressed similar to himself, in shorts, running vest and fell-running shoes. Dutch stopped and spoke to the individual, who was in the process of repairing the once solid stone barrier. The craftsman introduced himself as Peter Bidmead, an ex-traffic cop who had coincidently moved his dry-stone walling business from the Sussex coast to a larger business audience that existed around the fells and lakes of Cumbria. Due to the interest that Dutch showed in his work, he explained that he had a long interest in archaeology, and on retiring from the police some ten years before he had since gained a BA (Hons) and an MA in landscape studies and archaeology, which had then led him into his current career. The words, *ex-police from Sussex,* at first troubled Dutch, but he felt a sense of relief on realising that Peter would have been long retired by the time his own problems had begun. During their conversation it transpired that when Dutch was a young soldier they had competed against each other in cross country services races. Dutch also noticed that Peter's vest exhibited the logo of the local Ambleside running club, an organisation that he had eventually planned to join. Before Dutch departed from the man, whom he found to be very pleasant and interesting company, both arranged to not only meet at the athletic clubhouse that night, but Peter also invited Dutch to join him at a later date for some instruction into the intricate work and techniques of dry-stone walling.

During the remainder of his run, the conversation had given Dutch serious thought that during the quiet winter period when there were fewer tourists visiting the area. Therefore, there was less money to be earned following Peter's instruction; and when he was proficient enough to build and repair some of the many stone walls himself, this could provide him the necessary income to tide him over the winter months. On joining the fell running section of the athletic club, Dutch soon made many friends and proved to be a formidable runner in his age category over some of the toughest terrain in the country, which suited his competitive spirit, where he could test himself against both humans and nature. Every opportunity he got, rather than using a motor vehicle, with the use of a detailed map and his newly acquired mountain cycle he would investigate the more obscure and remote areas in search of the unusual to show his potential passengers. In his quest to stay fit and active within his new community, he also joined the local volunteer mountain rescue team, which again suited his adventurous spirit. The whole family were pleased and content with the move north. His father in law, Ken, enjoyed fishing nearly every day, and was spoilt for choice in which waters to fish. Molly had joined various women's leisure groups and was also constantly busy in her hobby of making her own greeting cards. Melanie was receiving great pleasure from her teaching role, especially as the younger child population of the village was small, meaning that she had more time to give individual help to those children who needed it. Even Jodie appeared happier in her new surroundings; although, the family had to keep an eye on the dog, as being a Collie she had a natural tendency to want to herd the numerous flocks of sheep scattered around the hillsides. If Jodie had been a younger dog, Dutch would have taken up a secret lifetime ambition, of training a dog to obey the instructions of a whistle, enabling them to enter sheepdog trials.

Dutch felt a proud man on the day that he received his brand new sixteen-seater customised minibus, bearing the blue and green coloured livery which, assisted by a remark made by Jon, he had designed himself. He then without delay obtained his obligatory operator's licence and was ready for business.

As the summer months were passing quickly it was essential that he started his advertising campaign immediately, and during the wait for his minibus he had employed an advertising agency to design a website to his specifications. The package that he purchased also included his business exposure on all the relevant social media sites, but to avoid his past problems his surname did not appear on any digital or printed material.

Dutch informed the company that he was now open for business, which led them to then activate their final procedures to reach the targeted audiences. While waiting for any results from the campaign, Dutch, together with Melanie and his in-laws, visited many of the surrounding towns and villages, which included cafes, tea rooms, bed and breakfast establishments, hotels and shops, distributing cards and leaflets about his new business. The visits revealed that many other similar companies were advertising in the same way, but Dutch was not disillusioned by this, as he had always been aware that the competition was fierce, but he was sure that he had the energy and tenacity to make his new venture a success. Business was slow at first, but he had not expected to be in constant work during what was the end of his first summer season. Between bookings he would carefully scour the lakes for the best photographic vantage points, and he took the opportunity to read all types of literature concerning the places of interest and the history of the area, not only to impart the knowledge to his potential passengers but also for his own personal interest. He also took time to visit and evaluate some of the shops and hostelries for his potential clients, and whenever possible holding a friendly meeting with the business owners. At the end of the school holidays there was a noticeable difference in the type of clientele visiting the area. Instead of family groups which had often included children, he was now carrying a greater number of couples only, or small parties of adults, some wishing a more peaceful experience and being grateful for avoiding the younger more boisterous tourists, or simply those looking for cheaper out-of-season accommodation.

As the autumn season approached and the leaves on the trees started to change colour, the Lakes and the surrounding area took on a different form of beauty. This was the time that Dutch was preparing to wind down the tour business for the winter period and prepare for the more strenuous employment of stone walling. Bookings for all similar tour operators were now few and far between, so he was grateful while sitting at home reading one Friday evening to receive a tour booking from the receptionist at the nearby Langdale Hotel and Spa for the following morning for a party of six. This was a welcome addition to the two persons who were already booked with him, and it meant that even without an afternoon tour he would still make good money, even after the respective agents had subtracted their commission.

Dutch awoke early, and although he never let his pride and joy remain dirty, he still washed and hoovered the tour bus to create a good impression to all of his clientele.

Having driven the short distance to the prestigious hotel, he reported to the reception desk and then returned to his transport to await his passengers. It had just started to rain heavily so when six women of various ages emerged from the front of the hotel they hurried to the nearby minibus covering their heads in various forms, protecting themselves from the rain. As they reached the vehicle Dutch opened the side door, allowing them all to enter quickly. Once they were all settled in their seats and once the excitement of their dash had subsided, Dutch from his driving position announced over his microphone headset that after collecting two further passengers from a guest house in the town centre, he would commence his wet weather tour. This consisted of visiting beauty spots and places of interest where it was not essential to leave the vehicle; although, if they wished to step outside he did carry a number of umbrellas in the luggage rack. After this, he would then take them to a typical Lakeland village where there were several small shops and tea rooms, after which hopefully it would have stopped raining and he would proceed to locations better suited for outside viewing and the taking of photographs.

Having located the two potential passengers in the town, he explained his same intentions to them, and the couple both approved of his planned journey. In the first part of the tour he took them to a vantage point on Coniston Water and explained how Sir Donald Campbell had met his death there when attempting to break the water speed record in 1967. He then proceeded to visit a number of properties once inhabited by famous artists, authors and poets including the former homes of author Beatrix Potter and poet William Wordsworth, one of a group known as the lake poets, all of whom had made literary contributions in describing the beauty of the area. As the rain eased Dutch made his way to the village of Grasmere, where all the passengers started to slowly disembark to visit the nearby shops and tea rooms. As the passengers began to walk from their transport, Dutch opened his map to plan the continuation of his tour, and he was about to open his flask of coffee when a woman he recognised through the rain affected glass as being one of his tour party knocked on the window of the front passenger door. Dutch, thinking that she had probably left something behind in the vehicle by mistake, or had a query regarding the remainder of the trip, indicated for her to open the unlocked door. As she did so, she said in an educated, soft north of England accent, "Hello, Dennis, how's the building work going?"

Dutch was puzzled by her question. She would obviously know his name as he had introduced himself when first addressing the two groups, but why would she mention building work?

There was something familiar about her and her voice. Then it dawned on him and he could feel his face immediately colouring up, and in an effort to prevent his anxiousness showing, carried out his regular routine when put in difficult situations by discreetly wiggling his fingers and toes. It was Kerry, the only indiscretion during his long marriage to Melanie. It had been a one-night romance when in his twenties they had met in a Warrington pub when he had reluctantly attended a fellow soldier's stag night, and she was entertaining some of the staff of her locally owned boutique. They had befriended each other when their respective parties were all drinking and they were not, and as neither he nor Kerry wished to get inebriated they went for a meal together. Although, they had only just met they had got on very well together, resulting in them both returning to Dutch's hotel room and engaging in a night of rampant sex; of which Kerry, unlike the inexperienced Dutch, appeared to be an expert exponent. They had spent the entire night together, after which Kerry had left for work the following morning, and they had not seen each other since. It suddenly dawned on him as to why she had mentioned building work. This was because prior to going on the stag weekend, the group of soldiers had, for security reasons decided to tell anyone who enquired that they were visiting construction workers.

Dutch tried to gain some composure, at the same time thinking of the intimacy that they had both shared together, as he said in a somewhat flustered manner, "Kerry, it's nice to see you again after what must it be?" As he hesitated Kerry, without any thought whatsoever, interjected, "Twenty-one years."

"You have obviously got a good memory for dates."

"Yes, that's because the following year was very eventful in so many ways. I opened up a new fashion store in Manchester and married the man who I had split from when we met, and had a child. I was only kidding you when I mentioned you being a building worker, as I later found out that you were all in the army and didn't want anyone to know, and being a local girl I can appreciate why, as I can clearly remember the IRA bombings in the town."

Dutch then coaxed her to sit inside the cab, saying, "I can remember feeling guilty about saying that, but with all that was going on at the time we had to be careful."

"I noticed that up to a few years ago you were running really well."

Once again Dutch was momentarily rendered speechless, then after hesitation, "How could you possibly know that?"

"It's okay, I'm not a stalker. My son is a very good all-round athlete and runner, so I regularly look at the Power of ten website to follow his results, so knowing you were a runner I looked you up."

A further bemused Dutch then said, "How could you do that as you didn't know my surname?"

"It doesn't seem as if you know what else happened on the night we met. We weren't the only ones who got up close and personal. You obviously remember, Peter Fisher?"

"Fingers. Yeah he was there that night. Why?"

"Well Pete, or Fingers as you call him, was one of the less drunk in your party and later, after we had left, he and one of my girls started a long-term relationship. The girl Jenny, who still works for me, was in a very volatile relationship at the time and immediately fell for Peter, who was as keen as she was. The problem was that she feared that if her husband found out he would revert to violence, so she pleaded with Peter to keep quiet about their affair, and if you don't know about it, he obviously kept his end of the bargain."

"The crafty bugger. Nobody had a clue. In fact, when he left the army soon after that trip he disappeared off the face of the earth without so much as a by your leave. There was a rumour he was heading north, but that's all."

"Well the good news is that both of them are now happy with children, and I see them often."

"That's good. So I'm guessing that you knowing these things about me means at some stage Pete has mentioned my name?"

"Exactly. Without letting out our little secret, over a period, each time I met them I would craftily gain a bit more info about you. I even know about your bravery award, Congratulations."

"Thanks, but that's all in the past now. So what brings you to these parts then?"

"I could ask you the same. For me, this trip is a token of appreciation to some of my staff, similar to the event when we met. I've been sitting behind you trying to make up my mind if it was you or not. You haven't changed much and from some of the things you said, especially when you mentioned that you also run around the area, I was then certain. You didn't recognise me at first, did you?"

"To be honest no, but only because I had to hustle you all in quickly due to the rain, and ever since then you've been sitting behind me, but when you came to the window and spoke I knew who you were immediately. I couldn't pay too much attention to six lovely ladies anyway or I would have been labelled a perv."

Laughing she replied, "Considering our past encounter we'd better not talk about such things, had we? You have certainly had a radical change of career."

"I've always loved the outdoors and this area suits my wife and her parent's fine."

Kerry, at the same time as delving into her handbag, said, "Talking about families, would you like to see a photo of mine?"

She then handed him her mobile phone, pointing out each character on the displayed image and saying, "That's my husband Gerry's daughter, Abi, and that's Andrew who's twenty." As she left her finger resting at the side of her son's face, Dutch was struck as to how much facially alike they were. He looked at Kerry who was staring straight into his eyes, "He looks very much like you, doesn't he?" she said.

Dutch was dumbstruck as this impromptu meeting had already sprung up many surprises, and now he was trying to do some simple maths in his head regarding the date of their sexual encounter and the age of her son, Andrew. He soon deduced that he could have been his father, and the longer he looked at the photo the surer that he was, as it was almost like looking into a mirror.

She could see his confusion and didn't help at all when she remarked, "He's also a very good all-round athlete. I don't know where he gets it from, as neither Gerry nor I are at all sporty."

Dutch, who still closely followed the athletics scene, suddenly recognised Andrew.

"Is your surname, Barlow?"

"Yes, that's right, you obviously recognise him from somewhere?"

"Of course. He's an up and coming triathlete. I've read articles about him in athletics magazines and have seen him on the telly several times. If he continues his progression he will be an international soon."

"That's right, Andy's represented England at the event as a junior, but his ambition is to eventually run fast marathons."

Such news initially caught Dutch's interest, as he had run an extremely quick time of two hours eighteen minutes over the marathon distance himself when younger. Although, he was excited of the prospects of her son succeeding in an activity that he also immensely enjoyed, due to what was going on in his head this was not the time for him to discuss sport.

Dutch was in a state of confusion, as he had a distinct feeling that Kerry was intimating that he was, or possibly was, the father of Andrew, or was it just the way he was interpreting the conversation? It certainly wasn't the sort of question that he could suddenly ask Kerry, in case he had got the signals completely wrong. On the other hand, if he did ask the question regarding parentage and she confirmed he was the father, where would they go from there? After all that Melanie had been through with wanting to provide him with a family but having been unable to do so, such news would break her already fragile mental health caused by two miscarriages and then the rape. There were so many others to take into consideration, not least Andrew himself. There was Kerry's husband Gerry, was he aware that he may not be the father of Andrew? The couple's own daughter, Abi, and his in-laws would all be greatly affected by such news. All these thoughts made him quickly realise that for everyone's sake he must leave well alone, and if he was the father and it was never to be discovered, then the only person left with regrets would be himself. Dutch had always wanted children, but not being one to make excuses, he accepted that it was his own fault and he would have to move on without causing disruption to what were now two happy families.

He could remember that on that night in question they had unprotected sex on many occasions and he could vividly remember how hypocritical he felt when later in his service he would tell young soldiers under his command not to do the same in order to avoid both sexually transmitted diseases and unwanted pregnancies.

Dutch was deep in these thoughts when Kerry said, "If you want a proper catch up why not come to the hotel when you have finished work? You could have a drink or use the spa facilities, which include a lovely swimming pool and sauna."

For a woman in her early fifties she was as attractive as he could remember her twenty years before. Her hair and makeup were immaculate, her dress was more appropriate for a glamourous night out rather than a bus tour, exactly the image of how one would expect the owner of ladies' boutiques to look. Her appearance and personality, together with the thought of spending some time in a pool and sauna were so tempting, but he could clearly remember the guilt . that he had been left with after the last time he met Kerry. Melanie had been so loyal to him during their long marriage and he couldn't let her down again. It could be that Kerry did just want to socialise with him and nothing more, but knowing of her previous vast appetite for sex he could not take the chance, because if the circumstances arose he knew that he could be as weak as the next man.

Dutch was thinking of fictional excuses as to why he couldn't visit the hotel when one of Kerry's party returned to the tour bus, informing Kerry that her coffee was getting cold and the group wished to take a stroll around the village before resuming the tour.

As Kerry left the vehicle, Dutch took a deep breath and reflected as to what had happened in a very short space of time. The fickle finger of fate had just confronted him with not only having to relive his past unfaithfulness to his wife but also had now left him with the thought that he may have spawned a son of whom he had no previous knowledge. His mind was now all over the place and he needed time alone to think. The last thing he needed was to continue the tour, but he knew that he had no choice but to complete the journey.

Once all the passengers had returned he drove high into the hills, and onto a rough track above Grasmere lake, and throughout the journey he couldn't help himself continually looking into his rear-view mirror in which he could see Kerry, and each time he did so she was staring back at his gaze. Once parked he walked the group to some gaps in the trees where they could all see the magnificent sight of the lake below, which was now shrouded in sunlight. Dutch told the party that he considered that this particular view was his personal favourite in the entire area. After his passengers had taken numerous photographs Dutch resumed the tour, but because his thoughts were now concentrated on the recent revelations he was aware that his commentary was not up to his usual standard.

On returning to the hotel where Kerry and her staff were staying, Dutch in his usual manner opened a side door to allow the passengers to disembark. Kerry was the last out and as the rest of her party walked towards their accommodation she handed Dutch a tip to which, as she explained, all of the party had contributed. They briefly exchanged pleasantries and the longer he was in her presence the more regret he felt as he once again turned down her evening invitation. As he waved Kerry goodbye he was aware that he would never know if he had a son or not, and his only consolation would be to read about Andy's athletics career, with the occasional viewing of him on TV. He knew that such occasions were going to be hard to live with.

During the harsh winter months associated with the barren landscape, tour bookings were sparse, but with the occasional work of stone wall building Dutch was able to provide a reasonable income which, supplemented by his army pension and Melanie's regular wage still provided them with a good standard of living.

Dutch remained vigilant, always aware that the cartel may continue their quest for revenge, which caused him to rent a small barn on a nearby farm so that his distinctive minibus would not reveal the immediate area in which he lived. Before approaching or leaving the lock up he would always, without fail carry out anti surveillance techniques to evade or detect any possible followers. Even if driving his wife's or father-in-law's cars he would regularly observe the rear-view mirrors for any possible followers. On more than one occasion he had cause for suspicion but was mindful not to allow vigilance to turn to paranoia.

As the following spring approached, Dutch began to prepare for what was hopefully going to be a good season.

Once the van had been given its annual service, he visited all of the local businesses where he had placed his adverting material and spoke with the agents regarding the forthcoming year.

Dutch was further buoyed when Jon Shipway rang him to express his delight that both of the Fergusons had each gone down for 12 years. During sentencing the judge had stated that although they had been targeted by Stanescu and Gheata the term of imprisonment imposed on all the offences reflected their continual lifetime of crime.

His first full booking of the spring was a multicultural affair, consisting of a number of nationalities including Japanese and couples from both North and South America.

At the conclusion of what was a normal and uneventful tour, all of his passengers wished to disembark at the busy Lake Windermere information centre, where they had parked their cars. As the entire group alighted and congregated around the tour bus, an American in the group, who was a pleasant enough man and who had been loudly vocal throughout the tour, looked at Dutch and pointing to the signage displayed across the side of the tour bus, said in yet another loud voice, "Lucky's Lakeland Tours, is that you? Are you Lucky?"

Dutch, looking the man straight in the eyes, said, "I truly believe that I am possibly the luckiest man on the planet, I've already had more than my nine lives. So much so that I may even write some books about my life story and my many death-defying moments. Look out for them."

The enquirer replied, "I can see that you sincerely mean that. I hope your luck continues. Thanks for a wonderful informative tour. Goodbye." He then handed Dutch a £10 note, for which Dutch acknowledged his gratitude.

As the group prepared to disperse in different directions of the busy car park, two men who had not been on his tour, but who Dutch had noticed at other locations throughout the journey, approached the assembly and having appeared to have taken an interest in the conversation between Dutch and the American, strode up close to Dutch. One of the two leant his head forward and quietly whispered into Dutch's ear in an unmistakable Eastern European accent, "Too many people around today, Mr French, but eventually everyone's luck runs out."

Before Dutch could react in anyway, both men walked into the busy car park and he soon lost sight of them. On quickly thinking over the morning's tour, he was almost certain he could recall seeing one of the two men taking photographs close to his group when assembled around his minibus at Lake Thirlmere. He had no reason to question it at the time as it is the practice for most tourists to be continually photographing the area. Dutch was sure that they would now have a good image of both himself and his transport for future use. His immediate thought was as they were unable to carry out their mission that day, to expose themselves in this manner was to prove how quickly, despite his efforts they were able to locate him, and were now leaving him to sweat, to wonder where and when they would next strike.

Having lived and worked in Sussex all of his sixty-nine years, this is his second novel. Married to Carla for forty-six years, they have three children and four grandchildren.

His hobbies include running, cycling and listening to music. His most current pastime of writing crime fiction novels derives from a long and varied police career and his admiration for our armed forces.

Sincere Message from the Author

To all those with addictions, whether it be alcohol, gambling or drugs, go and seek help now. There are many dedicated and understanding people out there waiting to help you to help yourself.